THE WINTER WHITE HOUSE

Also by J.T. Holden

Fiction

True Son

Apple-polisher

Three Imaginary Boys

JB: Or The Unexpected Virtue of Being Swaggy

(also published as *The Curious Disappearance of JB*)

The Boys From Manchester

Poetry

Alice in Verse: The Lost Rhymes of Wonderland

Twilight Tales: A Collection of Chilling Poems

O the Dark Things You'll See!

THE WINTER WHITE HOUSE

J.T. HOLDEN

For Andy Cigallio,
my faithful friend,
one more story to tell

*In loving memory of
the two Daves of
Video City*

So show me family
All the blood that I will bleed.

— The Lumineers

1

The golden sun, shot with streaks of orange and red, slowly sank into the western horizon, and dusk began to fall. The road ahead stretched out long and narrow, with nothing but miles of deserted land on either side, but Dylan knew, like all roads, it would eventually lead to civilization. A place far away from the one he was leaving, a place where he could have a fresh start on a new day and never look back. Not ever.

He had packed only the necessities—jeans, T-shirts, socks, underwear, and a couple of warm sweaters for the cold desert nights that lay ahead. He had left behind the watches, the designer clothes, and the Italian shoes—a manner of dress which had always made him feel uncomfortable. The only thing of value he had taken was the black Tesla Roadster, which he hadn't paid for, but it was registered in his name, so it wasn't like stealing. He planned to trade in the car for something more practical as soon as he got far enough away. He didn't want anything reminding him of who he was or where he had come from.

The cash tucked into Dylan's duffel—nearly forty grand—was all his. He had won it on an unbelievable run at a craps table the night before he'd made the decision to take off. It had been a rig-up, of course—a payback for some high roller from Texas who had lost a fortune in the Verdoux, an exclusive high-stakes poker room on the mezzanine level of the casino. The high roller's young wife or mistress, a hot blonde with small tits but a nice ass and long legs, just kept throwing the dice until the high roller had recouped enough of his losses from the poker table to put a Texas-sized grin on his face, and then she sevened-out. The end of her long run met with equal parts applause and groaning. Dylan didn't take part in either; by that point, he had made his wad and cashed out. For anyone else, there would have been tax forms to fill out, but when you're the top dog's son, they just smile at you through the cage and ask what denominations you'd like, and you walk away with heavy pockets.

The money would tide him over until he found a job—working the field on a farm or repairing cars in a garage, painting, carpentry, anything that he could do with his hands. He'd only just turned twenty-one, and hard labor where you didn't have time to chat was precisely what he was looking for. He had never been much of a conversationalist anyway. Not that he wasn't capable of intelligent conversation (indeed he had led his high school debate team to victory at the Harvard Tournament in his senior year); he just hadn't met many people who were interested in intelligent conversation.

Dylan was driving into the sunset with the top down and the wind in his hair, just like a character in a movie—the kind with a happy ending—when his phone began to buzz.

He looked at the screen and debated picking up. If he let it go to voicemail, there would be a message. And after a few minutes, it would ring again. Same caller, with another message. And this would go on for the next hour or so; every ten minutes, like clockwork, until his message box was full. But that wouldn't stop the calls from coming in—same caller every time; same time every time; ten-minute intervals between each; ten after, twenty after, thirty after, forty after, fifty after. When you're dealing with someone who is OCD, you get to know the pattern, and further, you understand that it will not stop until you pick up.

Dylan accepted the call and put it on speaker. "Hello, Charlie." He hoped his greeting didn't sound as distant as he felt.

Charlie didn't seem to notice and went right into the reason for the call in his usual rapid-fire manner. "Dylan, where are you? Please tell me that you're on your way. Everybody's already here. There are so many people, all over the place, it's like a real frat party. There are people swimming in the pool—nobody's naked yet, thank God. I don't think I could handle that sort of humiliation—I don't have the body for skinny-dipping, you know that. I'm not like you. People would just laugh."

Charlie chuckled like it was all good, but Dylan knew better. His younger half-brother was built tall and narrow like their Grandpa Jake, and despite the self-deprecating chuckle, Charlie was very sensitive about his lack of bulk.

"But they're here!" Charlie went on, excitedly. "In the pool—*swimming*. And they seem really happy, like they're actually glad to be here, which is good—don't get me wrong—really good because I want them to be happy. But I'm worried because I think they think this is *your* party— which is fine, I don't mind that at all. As long as they came, and they're having a good time and drinking and swimming—not doing both at the same time, at least not to excess, because I don't know how to clean sick out of a pool, and Father would be very angry if he found out that somebody had gotten sick in the pool, which I suppose would have to be drained and scrubbed, and that would be an ordeal, which would only make Father angrier."

He chuckled again, a dangerous low chuckle deep in his throat, and then shifted right back to the point of his phone call.

"But anyway, they're here, and they look more like you than me—I've honestly never seen so many beautiful people in one place. I mean, like really beautiful people, the girls *and* the guys, they look like fashion models come to real life. Please, tell me that you're coming, Dylan."

"Look, Charlie," Dylan said, gazing at the darkening road ahead, "there's something I need to talk to you about—"

"You can do it here!" Charlie cried excitedly. "It's perfect because I have something I need to talk to *you* about! The guests are all downstairs—at least, I think they are. Father would be most upset if any of them were up in the rooms, cavorting. But they're probably not. And if they are, we can go up there and clear them out together, and then we can have our talk in private. Please say you'll come, Dylan, please."

Dylan hesitated. Charlie waited with uncharacteristic patience. Dylan released a silent sigh; the urge to hang up and pitch the phone out onto the side of the deserted road was nearly irresistible.

Then Charlie said, "I feel so out of place here." His voice was reduced to a near-whisper. "I know they only came because they thought you'd be here. Everyone's been asking 'Where's Dylan?' over the past hour, and I keep telling them you're on your way."

Dylan's grip on the phone loosened, and he swallowed the lump in his throat.

Charlie went on in that same diminished tone. "I'm all elbows and knees, as Father says. I'm not like the guys here. I know that, I can see that. I know I'm a troll—"

"You're not a troll," Dylan said bluntly. He hated it when Charlie berated himself, almost as much as he hated it when the old man berated Charlie.

4

"You're just saying that because you have to," Charlie said, "because you're my older brother, even if we don't have the same mother. I can't help it that my mother wasn't a Swedish underwear model. Father usually has much higher standards and never mates below a seven. I can't help it that my mother was a four, at best—the only conclusion I can draw is that she must have gotten him drunk and taken advantage of him—you know he has no tolerance for alcohol, you know that, Dylan—I wouldn't have put it past her. Father is a man of considerable means and has been the target of many a gold digger in his time—"

Dylan's grip on the phone tightened again as he cut his younger brother off. "Your mother wasn't a gold digger, Charlie. She never took a dime from him."

"I know that," Charlie said, suddenly cowed and apologetic. "I know she wasn't like that. I was just pointing out that *other* women—nasty women, you know—women like that would soak an important man like Father to the bone. They'd prey on his kind nature and generosity and soak him right down to the bone if given half a chance. But you're absolutely correct. My mother was a good woman. A very good woman, and she would never do something like that. Never. I know it. She would sooner slit her own . . . you know . . . than do something like that—" Charlie abruptly stopped, as if he could feel Dylan's jaw tensing over the phone. Then in a sheepish tone, he said, "I didn't mean it like that. You know that, right, Dylan?"

Dylan stared through the Roadster's windshield, his features frozen into a hardened mask. He had kicked and kicked at the bathroom door until the lock had finally given way, and then he had raced straight to the tub. The water was already dark red, but he had wrapped her wrists in towels, all the time saying, "Stay with me, Charlotte, come on, stay with me." While dialing 911 on his mobile phone, he had caught sight of Charlie standing in the open doorway, staring at the scene with a numb expression on his pale face. And then the operator had come on, asking, "What's your emergency?"

"It's my . . . stepmother—" He had wanted to say 'mother' because she had loved and cared for him as if he were her own. "There's been an accid—" His voice had caught in his throat, and he had forced himself to continue. "There's a lot of blood, and I don't think she's breathing. Please send someone right away." Then he had turned to his little brother and said, "Charlie, look at me. Look at me." But Charlie's gaze had been fixed on the tub, where his mother's pale arm hung over the side, wrapped in a white towel that would have to be trashed—there was simply no way Lupita would be able to get out all of that blood. They had been thirteen and nine, Dylan and Charlie, at the time of Charlotte's death.

"Dylan," Charlie said now with a touch of fear creeping into his voice. "You know I didn't mean it that way. Please tell me you know that."

Dylan closed his eyes for a second, pushing back on the instinct once again to pitch the phone from the car and put the accelerator to the floor.

"Please, Dylan," Charlie said, with real emotion in his voice now. "Despite all of her problems, she was my mother, and I loved her, you know that I loved her."

He had almost said "shortcomings" instead of "problems," and he was glad that he hadn't. Dylan was a good person with the capacity to forgive almost anything. But a direct shot at the woman who had cared for him since he was four years old would most certainly press the far limits of his noble nature.

"Please, Dylan," Charlie pleaded, "tell me you know I didn't mean it that way."

Dylan opened his eyes and, gazing at the road, forced himself to respond. "It's all good, Charlie. I know you didn't mean it that way."

But that wasn't really true, because Dylan wasn't so sure about his younger brother anymore. On the surface, Charlie was a good kid—frequently awkward and occasionally inartful in speech, but still a good kid, trying, if not always succeeding, to be the best he could be. But there was a streak of the old man in Charlie, too; a propensity toward impulsive, often incendiary rhetoric that never failed to set Dylan's nerves on edge. And it had become more and more of a challenge for Dylan to hold his tongue when Charlie released a little of the verbal venom that their father spewed on a daily basis with zero regard for anyone's feelings.

Still, they were brothers, and unlike their older siblings, neither had entered the public spotlight of their father's shit show, and therefore, both still had a chance to walk away, unscathed. Dylan wanted this more than anything; he had actually considered taking Charlie with him on this one-way trip out West. But Charlie was still a minor and was always accompanied by at least two of the old man's bodyguards.

Dylan had had his own security detail when he was a kid, and though he'd been quite adept at giving them the slip, they'd always caught up and brought him home. They were very good at their job—so good, in fact, that if Dylan *had* taken Charlie with him this evening, both boys would be at Largo Morta right now waiting to have a video conference with the old man.

At least this would have been the outcome before the election. But now Dylan wasn't so sure.

The goon squad would have taken Charlie straight back home; that was a certainty. But Dylan himself might not have gotten off so easy. The old man's mood had been far darker than usual after his crushing defeat in both the popular vote *and* the electoral college last month. It had been a brutal loss, made worse by the fact that his opponent had been none other than Caitlyn Price, the granddaughter of Hannah and Blake Crichton. With the old man's temper still set on "seek and destroy," Dylan had no trouble imagining him turning his frustration and ire on his second youngest son and demanding he be charged with kidnapping his sixteen-year-old younger brother.

They had already quarreled over this matter back when the old man had first hit the campaign trail with his fiery rhetoric and brutal attacks—aimed at his Republican opponents as well as the most likely contender to win the Democratic nomination. The old man's crazy vitriol won him the Republican nomination. But it had little impact on Caitlyn Price, who turned out to be a far more beloved candidate than her grandmother had been forty years earlier.

Charlie had only been fourteen when the old man declared his candidacy for the Republican nomination. Kids at school, who had previously only snickered among themselves when Charlie walked by in the hallways, had become more aggressive. Inflamed by the daily doses of the old man's venomous oratory, both in the news and on social media, they had started to leave crass notes and newspaper clippings on Charlie's locker; spitballs were shot at the back of his head in class; shoulders slammed into him in the hallways; legs found their way into aisles as he headed to his desk; one particularly hostile kid stepped up to his table at lunch and, looking Charlie directly in the eye, spat in his food. And all of this had happened at a private school.

Things had finally come to a head when Charlie came home from school with a black eye. Dylan approached the old man in the office suite at Tower K in New York. It had been a closed-door meeting, but like most meetings with the old man, things eventually escalated and everyone in the outer office and adjoining hallway got an earful. Dylan said he wanted to take Charlie away, just until after the election; they could hire private tutors for him. Already loaded for bear and eager to fire at anything that moved, the old man saw a perfect target in his upstart nineteen-year-old son.

"The kid stays here," the old man said with finality. "Time for him to grow a pair and man-up. Running away from a fight never solved shit."

"This isn't *his* fight! He's *fourteen!*"

"Don't kid yourself. This is everybody's fight. Believe me. He's more than old enough to take one for the team. It'll toughen him up for the real world. You just worry about your own problems, like getting your degree and standing on your own two feet like I did, OK? Let me worry about the heavy lifting. That's what I'm here for, OK? You got that, Mr. Two Years Of College Under His Belt And He Suddenly Knows Everything, OK? Believe me, the kid's fine."

"That's the problem," Dylan shouted. "He *isn't* fine. Because all the crazy shit that's leaking out of your screwed up head is spilling all over him. Do you get that? Is there a crack in that thick skull of yours that the truth can seep into? He's *not* fine. You want to sit here building your house of cards, that's your business. But I'm not going to stand by and watch him get buried with you when it all comes crashing down. I'm taking him with me."

"Over my dead body."

The room had fallen deathly silent, and in that silence, Dylan's gaze bore into the old man as they stood eye to eye. Then in a quiet and cool tone, Dylan said, "Do you want to go there with me? How fast do you think your guys out there are? Do you think they can break through that door before I can test how well *you* can man-up?"

The old man had eyed Dylan like a cornered lion past its prime, and in that moment, in those faded eyes that had once been so fearsome, so terrifying, the son had seen the first chink in the father's armor. It hadn't made Dylan feel good, though; it had sickened him. And in the end, it had been a hollow victory because Charlie had chosen to stay with their father. And the old man hadn't even cajoled him. Charlie had looked Dylan in the eye and told him that he wanted to stay and begged him not to be angry.

Dylan hadn't been angry with the kid. He had been dismayed and confused, and a little hurt, but not angry.

Why the old man's faithful followers chose to remain with him, regardless of the insane crap he spewed, had been a mystery Dylan had long since given up on trying to solve. But this had been different. It wasn't millions of fans who had no clue what it was like to live with the old man. It was Charlie, who had lived in the eye of the storm his entire life, and he had chosen to stay with their father.

Dylan was surprised at how much that memory still hurt. The two of them standing together in the foyer, hugging each other as if for the last time, even though Dylan was only going off to college for his junior year and would be back during Christmas break. He could still feel Charlie's face buried against his chest, and he could hear the words spilling out between muffled sobs. "Please, don't be mad at me, Dylan, please don't be mad at me."

Dylan had held his brother tightly and spoken softly and gently, "I'm not mad, buddy. I could never be mad at you. OK? I love you, OK?"

But the most indelible memory was the image of the old man standing there, watching them hug goodbye. Though his expression was solemn—almost apathetic—there was a bright sheen in the old man's eyes that Dylan recognized at once. It was the glimmer of the victor—the old man's patented "screw you" look, the one that conveyed his favorite saying: *You mess with the big bull, punk, you'll get the horns every time.*

"Dylan, are you still there?"

Dylan snapped out of the memory and said, "I'm here."

Charlie chuckled nervously. "I thought I'd lost you for a minute there." He paused and then added, "Where are you? It sounds like you're in a wind tunnel."

"I'm on the road," Dylan said.

"Jeez, it's loud. Where are you headed?"

Dylan hesitated. "Nowhere . . . I've got the top down. Where are you?"

Charlie laughed. "At the party, silly, remember? Are you all right?" His tone shifted and became suddenly concerned. "Did I call at a bad time? Please tell me it's not a bad time—"

"It's not a bad time."

Charlie released a sigh of relief. "Oh, thank God because I really need you to be here, please tell me you're not far away—you're not on the highway, are you? You're not headed back up North, are you? Please tell me you're not . . . I can't . . . Please tell me that you're not . . . Tell me that, at least, please . . . "

"I'm not headed up North," Dylan said, truthfully. He took a silent breath and added, "Look, Charlie, that's what I wanted to talk to you about—"

"Then talk to me about it *here*," Charlie nearly keened. "Come here, and we'll talk. We can talk as long as you like. Just don't . . . just . . . don't do this over the phone, OK? Just please . . . " He swallowed hard, and a shaky wave of scarcely concealed emotion crept into his voice. "Just come, please, Dylan. Don't do anything until we've had a chance to talk . . . and then you can do whatever you like, I promise, whatever you like. I won't try and pressure you. I promise, no pressure. Just this one time, for me, please say you'll come, please."

Dylan took another breath, long and silent, and then responded gently, "OK, I'll be there."

"Soon . . . please."

Dylan looked at the odometer. He was only twenty miles out, and it wouldn't take long to backtrack. He gazed at the last glimmer of light on the horizon and said, "Yeah, Charlie, soon."

2

The seasonal lights of Largo Morta, the grand Spanish-style structure atop the highest point on the sprawling grounds, shined like ambient beacons in the darkness as Dylan's sleek black Roadster pulled through the main gates and headed up the long and winding driveway. Looking at the side view of his father's prized home away from home, Dylan couldn't help thinking that, save for the holiday decorations, nothing ever changed here. It was a beautiful place and far more tasteful than the New York penthouse or the ostentatious offices several floors below. But as with any of his father's countless other properties, Dylan never felt at home here. There was something about Largo Morta that made it feel less like a place for the living and more like a place where they put you on display before your interment. Morgana, the old man's latest wife (and second longest marital partner), had done her best to make it warm and welcoming, but she'd failed to vanquish the overhanging pall of the mausoleum that Dylan would forever associate with Largo Morta.

A sudden chill washed over Dylan as he rounded the generous curve of the winding drive just before it straightened into the final stretch that would take him to the main entrance. Off to his left, stood the massive hedge maze he remembered from his childhood. The walls, which rose ten feet high, were presently adorned with Christmas lights along their neatly trimmed tops. In the fall, the white bulbs were replaced with orange ones; in February, they were red for Valentine's Day; in March, green for St. Patrick's day. But, save for Memorial Day, the Fourth of July, and Patriot Day, when the lights were red white and blue, the vast configuration of interlocking hedges on the east end of the property stood in darkness during the spring and summer.

Dylan's foot eased off the accelerator as he gazed out at the maze and recalled the warm summer night back when he was eleven and Charlie was seven. Charlie had snuck out of the house after hours and got himself lost in the labyrinthine maze. Dylan had been sound asleep when his mobile phone began to buzz on the bedside table. Still half asleep, he'd reached over to switch off the ringer, but just before he did, an odd sensation passed over him. When he looked at the screen and saw his little brother's name, he accepted the call and said in a groggy tone, "Charlie, do you know what time it is?"

Charlie's response had come in a frightened whisper. "Dylan, I'm lost, and I can't find my way out." His breath came in quick, short waves, punctuated by whistling wheezes, like a tea kettle not quite at full boil. "I'm lost, and I can't—"

Dylan sat bolt upright in bed, his heart suddenly thundering. "Where are you?"

"I—" Charlie stuttered. "You can't get mad."

"Charlie—"

"You have to promise not to get mad."

"I'm not gonna be mad," Dylan said, trying to still the rising alarm within, but Charlie's wheezing was getting worse. "Charlie, do you have your inhaler? Use your inhaler. And do the breathing exercise Dr. Cathy taught you."

"I don't—" Charlie gasped. "I dropped it, and I can't find it in the dark."

Dylan's heart stopped. Then he leapt out of bed and pulled on his jeans while talking as calmly and quietly as possible. "You need to tell me where you are right now . . . Charlie, can you hear me? Tell me where you are."

An excruciatingly long moment of silence passed before Charlie's voice came back in a whimper. "You'll get mad . . . I know I'm not supposed to, and you'll be so mad at me . . . "

Dylan forced himself to speak calmly and gently. "I swear I won't be mad. Just tell me where you—"

Dylan stopped abruptly, and his eyes darted to the window, which overlooked the east end of the property, and suddenly he knew. Charlie had been fixated with the maze ever since their grandmother had shown them the model she'd commissioned from a famous French landscape architect. Children were forbidden to enter the maze without supervision, but that had never stopped Charlie looking upon the high arched entrance with a quixotic longing in his eyes. Dylan had done his best to divert his little brother, but when Charlie set his mind to something, he would eventually find a way to get it.

"Father is going to be . . . so angry," Charlie sobbed between wheezes.

"Stay exactly where you are," Dylan said as he slipped out of his bedroom as quietly as possible and made his way down the long hall. "I'm coming—just me. Nobody will ever know but us. I promise. Now breathe slowly and keep calm. Charlie, can you hear me?"

"I'm sorry, Dylan," Charlie whimpered. "I didn't mean to—"

"I know, buddy, everything's all right. But you have to stay calm, OK?"

"OK," Charlie's voice came in a strangled whisper.

Dylan took the back stairwell down to the kitchen in his bare feet. He found Charlie's spare inhaler in the cabinet above the sink and slipped quietly outside. The moment the night air hit his face, he broke into a full sprint toward the entrance of the maze.

It was a starless night and much darker inside the maze than Dylan had expected. Even with his phone's flashlight, it was difficult to navigate the myriad twists and turns and backtracks from dead ends. He kept talking to Charlie the whole time, but Charlie's answers became shorter and less coherent with each passing minute, and before long, a cold shaft of panic crept into Dylan's consciousness. If he didn't find his brother soon, he would have to alert security, and that would mean the old man would find out. And then all hell would break loose, followed by a lecture that would likely last till dawn—there was nothing the old man enjoyed more than berating those who triggered his ire, and once he got going, you were in for the duration.

After a full five minutes of searching—which felt more like five hours—Dylan was ready to damn the consequences and call in the security team. When they alerted the old man, Dylan would make up a story; tell him that they had been playing hide and seek and that Charlie had gotten lost. The old man would look to Charlie for confirmation, and under the pressure of that imposing gaze, Charlie would crack and tell the truth. This wouldn't get Charlie completely off the hook, but it would shift the lion's share of their father's anger away from Charlie and onto Dylan for lying about the reason he and his brother were up so late and fooling around in the maze. While the old man spoon fed a daily diet of deception and outright lies to family, friends, and followers alike, he had no appetite for bullshit—especially bullshit served up by one of his children.

Dylan was about to tell Charlie to hold on while he switched over to call the security team when inspiration suddenly struck. Well, not exactly inspiration, Dylan thought;

more like common sense. He quickly flipped through his phone's screens until he found the Friend Finder app. He turned it on and walked Charlie through the steps to activate the same app on his phone. It took a moment, but soon, a map appeared on Dylan's screen, along with a pulsating red dot, indicating that Charlie was at the east end of the property. Dylan refined the parameters, shrinking the search zone to encompass only the maze. And then he followed the pulsating red dot on the screen until the blue dot, which indicated his own location, caught up.

Charlie was lying on the dewy grass in an alcove deep in the maze. His skin was pale, and his breath was coming in frightfully shallow waves. Dylan knelt at once, shook the inhaler, and put it to Charlie's mouth. It took only two deep pulls to open the constricted airway, and once Charlie was breathing, Dylan took his younger brother into his arms and held him tightly as the boy sobbed, "I'm sorry, I won't do it again, please don't tell Father."

"Shhhh," Dylan said, holding him tighter, "I won't tell anyone, I promise, shhhh."

And he hadn't told anyone. Not even Charlotte—mostly because he hadn't wanted to frighten her. Charlie had come away from his spooky after-hours adventure in the maze unscathed, and that was all that mattered.

But Dylan had been smart enough not to leave it at that. He knew Charlie too well. Eventually, the fright would fade and the curiosity that had led him into the maze after hours would return. So, the following day, he took Charlie back to the maze—accompanied by Fernando, who was Lupita's cousin and the second assistant groundskeeper at Largo Morta. Together, they mapped out the entire maze. It took over six hours, but Fernando, who otherwise would have had to spend the day with the grounds crew, trimming out the rough, thorny growth at the west end of the property, didn't mind the diversion. And when they'd finished,

Charlie had a map on his mobile phone that would prevent him from ever getting lost inside the maze again.

Dylan released a short breath as he rounded the final curve of the long driveway, and the maze disappeared from view. The fork ahead split into two different directions—one leading to the opulent guest entrance up front; the other winding around back to the family residence with its private parking and equally opulent entrance.

The residence took up one-third of the hotel's east wing. To keep guests from accidentally—or intentionally—entering this restricted area, the connecting hallway could only be accessed with a high-security key card. Dylan's key card was in his wallet. He had planned on mailing it to the concierge during his first overnight stop on the way to California, but now that he was here, he would just leave it on the dresser in his room after his talk with Charlie. He certainly wouldn't be needing it after tonight.

The guard at the small gatehouse recognized Dylan's Roadster and waved him in without checking his ID. The old man would have pitched a fit at the breach of security etiquette, but Dylan, who was no longer concerned with the old man or his fits, just gave the guard a friendly nod as he passed by and continued to the residence.

Normally on the eve of a major holiday, the residence entrance would be manned by at least three valets to park the cars of family members and VIPs, but with the old man and Morgana out of the country, there was only one—a handsome eighteen-year-old, dressed in black trousers, a matching vest, a crisp white shirt with a smartly knotted black tie, and a name tag that read BETO. He came down the steps with a big smile as Dylan pulled to a stop.

Dylan extended his fist. "You got a promotion."

"Movin' up," Beto said as he bumped Dylan's fist.

"My old job," Dylan said. "Which, now that I think about it, isn't much of a promotion."

Beto grinned. "Yeah, but it's got the sweet tips, jefe."

"Yeah, but you gotta be around front to *get* 'em, hermano. What are you doing back here? The pricks that come this way don't even tip half the time. Have you met my older brothers?"

Beto laughed.

Dylan shook his head. "You know I can just park this myself. I know where it is."

Beto grinned sheepishly. "You tryin' to get me fired on my first day?"

Dylan rolled his eyes with an exaggerated sigh. "That explains why you're back here. All right," he added, unbuckling his seat belt and getting out of the car. "Just try not to ram it into a tree back there." He gave Beto the valet key and another fist bump and headed toward the door.

"Which side do you want the scratch on?" Beto called out as he got behind the wheel.

Dylan's response came without hesitation. "The left, hermano, always the left." He was almost at the door when he stopped and turned back. "Hang on for a sec. What time do you get off?"

"Ten," Beto said. "Jerry's not letting anybody have their keys if they're too drunk, so he's coming on to do the late shift himself. Why? What's up?"

"Hang on." Dylan went back to the car, opened the trunk and rooted around inside his duffel. He found the envelope with the cash he'd won at the old man's casino and took out a bundle of fifty-dollar bills—he could make it on thirty-four grand and change just as well as he could on thirty-nine and change. He stuffed the envelope back inside the duffel, closed the trunk, and went around to the driver's side of the car.

"Here," he said, leaning in the open window with

his forearms on the door. He extended the wrapped stack of bills to Beto, who looked both confused and shocked. "Merry Christmas and Happy New Year."

Beto shook his head. "Oh, man, I couldn't—"

"Don't make me beg you," Dylan said with a smile, though there was a hint of sadness in his eyes. "Just take it."

"Seriously, bro, it's too much. I can't—"

"No," Dylan said, "actually, it's not enough. But I'm gonna need the rest for where I'm going, so this is the best I can do."

"Seriously, man, I couldn't—"

"Sure, you can," Dylan said with a wink. "I did. It's free money. I won it at the craps table the other night. Trust me; they're not going to miss it. Take it, man. You're gonna hurt my feelings."

The hint of sadness was still there in Dylan's eyes. But there was something else just behind that sadness, and it looked like hope. Still a bit uncertain, Beto took the cash.

"Now stick it in your pocket and don't take it out until you get home. And don't let anybody know you've got it—they'll be your best friend until the last nickel is gone. Use it for school. You're in college now, right?"

Beto nodded. He'd just started his freshman year at the University of Miami on a partial scholarship. His mother had taken out a loan and was working extra shifts in house-keeping to ensure that he would get a good education and become someone.

"What's your GPA?" Dylan asked.

"Three-point-eight."

"Outstanding. How'd you do on your first semester finals?"

"Aced them."

Dylan's eyes narrowed suspiciously.

"All but one," Beto conceded with a guilty grin. "Game Theory—but it's an *elective*, jefe, so it doesn't really count."

Dylan shook his head, but he was smiling. "Yeah, but it'll count when you find yourself on the wrong side of the zero-sum."

"I don't believe in the zero-sum," Beto said. "I mean, I know it exists and that there are people who live by it who'll do whatever it takes to win. But I think the win-win is possible, and I think most people know it, you know?"

Dylan nodded, moved by the naked sincerity in Beto's eyes and wanting more than anything to believe that he was right. "Good deal," he said. "Keep the grades up. And don't let anybody distract you—the first year is filled with distractions. Just keep your nose in your books and your eye on the prize. Kids are gonna be dropping like flies all around you, but you stick to the plan."

Beto nodded, but suddenly he felt a wave of fear. Not for himself but for Dylan, who had always been kind to him and his mother. He hesitated and then asked cautiously, "Are you in trouble?"

Dylan looked up at the hotel, shook his head, and smiled that sad smile again. "I was born in trouble, hermano." He patted Beto on the shoulder with a gentle fist and said, "Tell your mom I said Happy New Year. And remember what I said about school, right?"

"I will."

"Good deal." He stepped back, thumped the trunk of the car twice, and headed for the entrance without looking back.

3

Dylan would have preferred to bypass the party altogether; just have his chat with Charlie in private and leave quietly without being noticed. But any hope of a stealthy in-and-out vanished the moment he stepped into the Atrium.

He'd expected the party to be contained to the Red Lounge, which opened onto the north patio, where the private pool was located, but apparently Charlie's New Year's bash was a much bigger event than he'd intimated in their phone conversation. There had to be at least a hundred guests here, and the overflow had spilled into the Atrium with its vaulted glass ceiling. (The Grand Atrium was an addition that Morgana had overseen shortly after she'd married the old man. It was completely incongruous with the Spanish architecture of the original structure, which had been built back in the 1920s, but Dylan thought it perfectly summed up the imbalance and ostentation of the family that had occupied the residential wing of Largo Morta since long before he was born.)

The vast area was decked out with gaming tables—craps, roulette, blackjack, baccarat, pai gow—and manned by dealers in evening dress. Waiters and waitresses served drinks on trays to teenagers and twentysomethings alike, without carding any of them. Laughter and cheering nearly drowned out the full-blast music spilling from the monster speakers at the four corners of the Atrium.

As Dylan passed through on his way to the Red Lounge, where he suspected he would find his brother, a few familiar faces from high school lit up with grins of acknowledgment; hands reached out to clap him on the shoulder, hugs came from pretty girls (one of these girls, a brunette with smoldering hazel eyes, who appeared to be well past her limit, kissed him on the lips and said with a grin, "I'm still not speaking to you!").

A rosy-cheeked, hefty guy named Phil Parma, who had been on the soccer team with Dylan back in high school, turned in his seat at a nearby blackjack table and extended his fist in greeting. Dylan bumped Phil's fist with his own and asked, "Have you seen my brother?"

Phil shook his head. "I saw him for like two seconds when I got here, but I haven't seen him since. He got tall. He used to be such a tiny little shit," Phil said with a grin and a chuckle, and he nodded at the empty seat next to his. "You playing? The dealer's running as cold as a corpse—" He shot a sly glance at the dealer. "—no offense. You're the best thing that's happened to me in my entire miserable life."

The dealer, a stunningly beautiful young woman with caramel colored skin and long, dark curly hair, smiled demurely. Phil chuckled and turned back to Dylan.

"She doesn't believe me," Phil said with a lazy grin. "But then she doesn't know that I work for your old man." Phil raised his glass in a mock toast. "Here's to a new year in the trench. When are you coming on board? You graduate in June, right?" Phil was a few years older than Dylan and had worked his summer breaks at Tower K in New York before graduating from Cornell and taking a full-time position in Dylan's father's company. He took a bracing sip from his glass of whiskey and added with a grin, "Your old man's a vindictive prick, but he can't resist a pooch with a pedigree, and, trust me, those Harvard bona fides go a long way with him. He salivates over shit like that. You're golden, and, as we both know, he can't resist anything that's golden. He'd lick a bull's nuts if it could shit gold bricks."

Dylan cracked a small smile in spite of himself. Phil had always been one of the few people who could get him to smile back in high school when the pressure of living under the old man's roof kept the happy moments to a bare minimum. Soccer had provided a release valve for pent-up steam (indeed on more than one occasion, Phil had had to pull Dylan off of another player when a fight broke out on the field), but it wasn't until he had gone off to college that Dylan felt he could breathe and let his guard down.

Phil grinned with narrowed eyes and devilishly arched brows. "There's that smile," he said with a chuckle. "Jesus, the men in your family are so tightly wound it's a wonder you don't all explode into a million pieces and come raining down in a shower of maudlin confetti."

Phil polished off his whiskey and signaled a passing waiter for another. Then he looked back at Dylan and said, "I know what you're thinking, and the answer is yes: He's still smarting over that interview with Grimley. He's pissed, but he'll get over it. You're family, and he wants you in the fold, even if you cross him at every turn—hell, he *thrives* on the conflict. A part of him *lives* to be challenged by you. It's like sustenance to him."

Dylan did not dispute Phil's claim. He knew the old man thrived on conflict—though, he wasn't so sure about the claim that his father liked being challenged by his upstart, free-thinking son. As far back as Dylan could remember, the only fight the old man enjoyed was the kind where his opponent was left crushed and bleeding beneath the heel of his Louboutin Greggo's.

Phil shook his head with a small, sly smile and a gleam of admiration in his glassy eyes. "Man, that took some balls—the old fucker went through the roof over that interview."

The "interview" Phil was referring to had taken place at Colin Grimley's Fastball College Tour during the election. Dylan hadn't planned to be there; a group of friends had dragged him along. It had been bad enough to watch his father spouting the usual crazy up on stage while he sat in the darkened auditorium, surrounded by his classmates. But the worst of it had come when Grimley took a live mic into the audience for a Q&A between the students and the candidate.

Dylan had tried to make himself invisible, but Grimley spotted him. Just like his predecessor and father—Chase Grimley, the original host of *Fastball* and the Fastball College Tour on NCMSB—Colin Grimley had a disarming smile and easy manner that belied the hard-nosed journalist beneath the friendly façade. And so Dylan had no choice but to stand up when Grimley said with a smile, "I think I recognize this handsome young fella—stand up so we can see you, Dylan. I'm sure everyone's dying to hear what question *you* have for the candidate!"

It hadn't been an intentional "gotcha" moment—though many on the far right claimed it was precisely that. But just the same, it ended up dominating the news cycle for nearly two weeks—a lifetime in politics—when Grimley asked a seemingly innocuous question of the candidate's son: "So, who're ya gonna vote for, Dylan? Your old man or Caitlyn Price—the granddaughter of your great-grandfather's arch nemesis, Hannah Crichton—who's it gonna be?"

The audience had chuckled as Grimley held the microphone out to Dylan, fully expecting the young man to say his father's name. But after several long seconds of silence, a ripple of low, spooky laughter rolled through the auditorium. No smile had come from either the candidate or his son. Dylan had just continued to stare at the old man, who gazed right back at him with a stony expression.

Grimley had attempted to save the day by calling out to the candidate with a good-natured chuckle, "I think you might still have some work to do with the younger voters here, Jake."

The old man responded with a thin smile, but his gaze had remained locked on his son, and the fire smoldering behind that gaze had been clear for all to see.

That had been back in April, months before the old man had sewn up the Republican nomination. But for a time, there had been serious doubt by pollsters and donors alike that the old man could pull it out. It went right up to the eleventh hour when New York finally put him over the finish line by a razor-thin margin with 1,239 delegates—just two more than the 1,237 needed to clinch the nomination.

Phil looked down at his drink and said, "Yeah, I'm sure he'll get over that in time . . ."

A moment of silence passed. Phil chuckled, Dylan smiled, though neither looked particularly amused.

"Well, we could definitely use you," Phil said with a sigh. "You're the only one with the balls to stand toe to toe with him—your older brothers are about as useful as a couple of eunuchs in a whorehouse—" Phil shot an apologetic glance at the dealer. "Excuse my French. I'm a Neanderthal, just ask my friend here."

The dealer didn't seem to mind. Phil swirled his drink absently. Dylan waited silently.

"The daily whine about getting cheated by 'Shady Hannah's granddemon' is very inspiring," Phil said with a chuckle. He dropped a wink and added: "I voted for your old man, but secretly, I was relieved when she beat him—no offense."

"None taken."

Phil halted, and his bleary eyes grew wider for a second before narrowing to near slits, and he chuckled again. "Oh my god. You voted for her, didn't you."

Dylan's face felt warm, but he didn't respond.

Phil clapped a hand to Dylan's shoulder and released a low, throaty chuckle of devious delight. "Sweet Jesus, you are a stone cold badass with a big brass set." He shook his head, still chuckling. "Well, whatever you do, keep that little nugget between us—your old man's batshit crazy pissed as it is, and that would probably send him so far over the edge that even your grandmother, with all her dark dowager powers, won't be able to reel him in." He patted the empty seat. "Come on, play a few hands with me. I'm lonely."

"Maybe later," Dylan said. "I need to talk to my brother first."

"All right," Phil called out as Dylan headed off. "But this run ain't gonna last forever, I can tell you that much." And then he turned back to the pretty dealer with the lovely dark curls and caramel colored skin and sighed, "Nothing lasts forever, does it?" He downed his drink and shoved another stack of chips onto the circle in front of him. "That's why I live for the moment."

4

The party was thumping in the Red Lounge, and more familiar faces greeted Dylan as he passed through, looking for Charlie. The tall speakers on the patio outside were blaring an old tune by The Offspring: *The Kids Aren't Alright*—a sentiment which Dylan could not refute. Through the long glass wall on the north side of the lounge, Dylan could see the private pool. Lit by colored lights and loaded with young people in bathing suits, it looked like something out of a movie—a high-gloss slasher flick, set at a posh resort, where you know that most of the cast will be dispatched in grizzly yet stylish fashion by the end, and at least one principal character will wind up floating face-down in that pool.

As a kid, Charlie had loved those glossy slasher flicks and would sit before the TV with rapt attention, never shying away or covering his eyes during the gory parts. He particularly liked the ones where a group of unsuspecting victims were invited to a remote location and killed off one by one until all that was left was the final two or three, and the killer was revealed to be one of them. But the endings were mostly downers for Charlie because inevitably the killer would be killed (by either the handsome hero or the beautiful heroine or both) before he could finish the job.

Dylan recalled Charlie turning to him after one movie and saying, "They need to make one where he gets them all."

Charlie couldn't have been older than ten at the time, and Dylan, who was only a teen and hadn't thought there was anything strange about his younger brother's infatuation with horror films, said with a tentative smile, "Yeah, but he got almost everyone—at least all of the assholes."

Charlie had looked thoughtful for a moment before responding in a carefully measured tone, "Yeah, but he didn't get them *all*. They should do one where he gets them all . . . where there's nobody left at the end, you know?"

Dylan laughed. "Man, are you bloodthirsty or what?"

Charlie smiled bashfully. "I just think it would be more interesting. It's boring when the hero always wins."

A few days later Dylan brought home a movie called *And Then There Were None*. It wasn't a teen slasher flick, and there wasn't much gore in it. But it did have a couple of fairly grisly deaths, and more important, it had precisely the sort of ending that Charlie had been craving. The killer got everyone, including the handsome "hero" and beautiful "heroine," so by the time the credits rolled, all that was left was a house filled with ten corpses and a mystery that couldn't be solved.

Dylan had never seen his kid brother so silent after a movie. Charlie just sat there, staring at the screen with a thoughtful expression on his solemn face. And just when Dylan was about to ask him what he thought, Charlie nodded and said softly, "I liked it. Thank you, Dylan."

Coming from any other kid, that response might have seemed a bit odd. But coming from Charlie, it had been perfectly normal. After that night, Charlie's fixation with slasher flicks had waned, and his interest had shifted to mysteries and thrillers—especially ones with a shocking twist at the end.

Dylan made his way through the throng of partygoers in the Red Lounge without getting held up by more than a few quick greetings from friends who hadn't seen him since high school. He paused only once, to bump fists with a guy named Xander Grach and ask if he'd seen Charlie. But Xander's response ("I think I saw him heading to the Atrium, but that was like a half hour ago—") fell on deaf ears because just then Dylan's eye was caught by a girl across the room. The lights were low in the Lounge, but Dylan had no trouble making out her features. She had lush auburn hair and dazzling green eyes, and when she looked in Dylan's direction, the ghost of a smile appeared to curl at the corners of her sensuous mouth.

Dylan stood very still as he tried to place her face with a name. But despite the effort, he kept drawing a blank. Still, there was something familiar about her, as if he should have recognized her at first glance.

The moment ended when Xander suddenly snapped his fingers and said, "Nah, I remember now. I saw him heading upstairs. He was talking with some hot girl, and then she whispered something in his ear—I remember that cuz I thought, 'Oh, yeah, Charlie's gonna get some *tonight!*'" He jabbed at Dylan's stomach playfully and grinned. "Just like his big bro, am I right?"

Dylan forced a smile and asked, "Are you sure he went upstairs?"

Xander nodded, sipping his beer. "Pretty sure. You want a brew?"

"Maybe later," Dylan said as he stole another glance at the girl across the room. But she wasn't looking at him anymore. She was engaged in a conversation with one of the others in her group, and it suddenly felt as if she'd never looked up and seen him in the first place.

Just off the Red Lounge was a long glass corridor which

connected the first floor of the residence to the hotel lobby. Dylan could still hear the muffled throbbing of the music coming from the Lounge as his footfalls echoed along the marble tiles. At the end of the corridor, there were three elevators, all with key card access only. Dylan's card (along with the cards of everyone else in the family, save for one) only worked with two of these elevators. The third was a private lift and could only be accessed with the old man's card. In the old man's reckoning, waiting for elevators was what other people did; when he swiped his card, he expected the doors to open at once.

Dylan assumed that his younger brother must be up in the Solarium, the quiet and dimly lit octagonal room at the top of the residence with glass walls that offered a stunning 360° view of the grounds.

The Solarium had always been Charlie's "safe place"—whenever he got upset about something and "ran away from home," Dylan could always count on finding him up there. And after he'd won Charlie's confidence and got him to reveal what had upset him enough to make him run away from home (usually something the old man had said or done), Dylan would coax his little brother to the windows with a sly grin and an enticing line like, "Man, you should see them going at it down there." This had never failed to bring Charlie around, and before long, they would be standing side by side at the window, watching while the staff—along with their two older brothers from the old man's first marriage—frantically searched the grounds for Charlie. They would stand there up in the glass-walled Solarium, Charlie and Dylan, watching and laughing until Charlie had forgotten all about what had upset him.

But that wasn't entirely true, Dylan thought now. As carefree and happy as Charlie had seemed watching the adults fumbling around the grounds in their clumsy effort to find him, he'd never really forgotten the offense that had precipitated his disappearing act. You could see in his eyes that the infraction, no matter how great or small, had been catalogued and preserved in his memory—particularly when the offending party was the old man.

Dylan recalled countless family dinners where Charlie sat quietly looking up from his plate at the old man cutting and chewing his rare steak, oblivious to the fixed gaze of his youngest son, deaf to the soft breath the boy would take and hold each time the chewing stopped and the swallowing began. And in that seemingly endless moment when the food was making its way from the old man's mouth to his stomach, Dylan too would hold his breath.

But, unlike his younger brother, Dylan's point of focus was never the old man. In these tense moments at the table, Dylan's gaze was always fixed on Charlie . . . the predatory gleam in the boy's eyes as he focused on the old man's jugular with the patience of a cat, following the movement of the muscles in that fleshy throat as they worked to push the lump of chewed meat down the esophagus. And only when the process was completed would Dylan release his breath, right along with his brother—though Dylan's release had always come with a sense of relief while Charlie's seemed to herald something closer to disappointment.

Most of the time, Charlie would turn back to his plate in short order, allowing Dylan to relax and go back to his own dinner. But sometimes, Charlie's fixation on their father's bobbing Adam's apple would last so long that Dylan, nervously watching from his seat, would become physically ill.

One time, the sensation was so powerful that Dylan threw up at the table.

This had occurred after a particularly bad pre-dinner blowup between Charlie and the old man. Charlie had wanted to join the old man on a trip to London because they were reading Dickens in his literature class at school, and he figured it would be enlightening to visit Dickens' old haunts. The old man had flatly said no, that it was a business trip and no place for a kid. Charlie countered by citing numerous business trips the old man had taken him on before, but the old man wouldn't budge. With no acceptable answer as to why he couldn't join their father on this particular trip, Charlie hacked into the old man's itinerary on his mobile phone and discovered that the trip wasn't to London at all; it was to Prague. Dylan had been standing outside of the study when Charlie confronted the old man about the lie shortly before dinner. The exchange was brief and ugly. The old man called Charlie a dirty little spy and threatened to ship him off to boarding school if he "ratted" him out to Morgana.

Charlie didn't spill the beans. He just sat at the table, gazing coldly at the old man all through the meal. Dylan supposed that it would have ended like any other family dinner. But when Charlie's slender fingers unobtrusively curled around the handle of his steak knife, Dylan's stomach lurched, and his resolve to keep his dinner down failed.

He'd tried to get up to make a run for the toilet but wasn't fast enough. The half of the dinner he'd already consumed came up in a steaming rush that splashed onto the table, soiling the gravy boat and the bread basket.

Morgana had been the first to react. She put the back of her hand to her mouth, turned her head to one side, and dry heaved. But to her credit, she did not vomit. The response from Dylan and Charlie's older half-brothers, who were sitting across the table, followed fast. Tom, who had been in the middle of swallowing, began to gag, causing bits of food to spray forth, while Brady spat out the food he was chewing and retched repeatedly into his napkin.

The only ones who didn't react were Charlie and the old man. Both sat perfectly still as if observing an innocuous anomaly like two characters in a surrealist painting.

The bizarre tableau lasted only a few seconds—though it felt much longer to Dylan, whose stomach was now empty but still trembling with spasms like tiny aftershocks of an earthquake. Then with a suddenness that drew a clipped, high-pitched sound of shock from Morgana and a frightened grunt from Brady, the old man slammed his silverware onto his plate, shoved his chair back from the table, and announced, "I don't eat with animals. I'm going out to get a burger."

Both Tom and Brady got up and followed their father out of the dining room—apparently, at least one of them thought he could join the old man on his burger run because Dylan heard an angry voice barking out in the hallway, "No, you stay here. You smell like vomit, and I don't want to smell vomit while I'm eating. It's disgusting."

Morgana made her exit shortly after, leaving the two youngest brothers alone at the table.

Dylan looked dazed. Charlie appeared sanguine. He patted Dylan gently on the shoulder and said, "Go upstairs and lie down, Dylan. Your color looks off. I'll tidy up down here and be up to check on you as soon as I'm done."

It had been odd, hearing his ten-year-old brother speak to him as if he, Dylan, were the younger one. But he had obeyed Charlie's gentle command, and as promised, a short while later, Charlie had come up to his room with a steaming cup of Chamomile tea on a tray with crackers. And after Dylan had finished the tea and crackers, Charlie stayed with him, speaking soft words of comfort—just as Charlotte used to do when one of them was ill and bedridden—until Dylan had fallen soundly asleep.

A sudden tingle ascended Dylan's spine as the memory of Charlie sitting beside his bed while he drifted off to sleep receded. Only this tingle wasn't the warm and fuzzy sort. It was more like an icy finger had touched the base of his spine, sending a wave of chilly tendrils racing up to the nape of his neck.

Dylan took out his key card and swiped it through the electronic lock. He was waiting for the elevator to arrive when a sudden sound echoed off the arched ceiling of the glass corridor, causing him to start and turn around fast. It was a deep sound, somewhere between a growl and a grunt, like the sound a bull makes when it shoots hot breath through its nostrils just before charging at the red cape.

The animal at the opposite end of the corridor was not a bull, but it was very large—nearly twice the size of an average shepherd, with huge paws, a massive head, and a long, sinewy body. It stood there for a brief moment, contemplating Dylan with its searing golden eyes.

Then, without warning, the massive beast sprang into action, bridging the distance in seconds and leaving Dylan with scarcely enough time to react. He raised his hands—to slow if not stop the charging animal—but it was too late. At the last second, the dog leapt up, its huge paws landing on Dylan's shoulders, and knocked him over.

As Dylan lay defenseless on his back, the dog pelted his face with kisses, and he laughed and ruffled the silky coat of fur while cooing, "Who is this guy? Who is he? He's as big as a pony, yes he is, yes he is! Hakhan is a very big boy, yes he is . . . "

Dylan was so absorbed in his reunion with the dog that he didn't hear the footfalls echoing down the marble floor. Nor did he notice the lovely girl smiling at him from across the hall. He only looked up when she spoke.

"Looks like love at first sight to me."

It was the girl from the Red Lounge, the one with the auburn hair and stunning eyes who had given him the appraising look from the dark corner of the room.

Dylan sat up and continued to pet the dog, but his eyes were on the girl now. "Nah, we're old friends. We just haven't seen each other in a few months, have we buddy?"

Hakhan pelted Dylan's cheeks with more kisses, and

the girl laughed; her smile was beautiful. "So it seems," she said with a nod. "Well, if you two want some alone time, I completely understand."

Dylan got up, and Hakhan immediately worked his head into Dylan's hand. "You don't have to go." He said it casually, but he really didn't want her to go. He looked into her lovely eyes and something about the way she looked back at him made him smile.

"Wow," she said with a delightful laugh, "you actually *can* smile." Dylan's cheeks flushed. "Don't be embarrassed," she added, "it looks good on you. Not that your brooding intense expression looks bad—it's very attractive in a dark and mysterious way—but your smile is better. You should do it more often."

Dylan's brow furrowed, but he was still smiling. "I know you, don't I?"

"For about five seconds," she said with a shrug. "I was a freshman when you were a senior. Well, technically, I *should* have been a sophomore, but my birthday is in November, and my mother had separation anxiety, so she held me back a year until I was 'legally' five and the oldest living Kindergartner. I looked a lot different the last time you would have seen me wandering the high school halls— shorter, flatter, less makeup, terrible fashion sense."

Dylan's smile receded as a sudden shaft of shame pierced him.

"Don't look so mortified," the girl chuckled, though not unkindly. "You were very nice. A perfect gentleman. You always gave me a smile and a nod when you caught me sneaking a peek at you—even when you were brooding— which was pretty much all the time."

Dylan's cheeks flushed a deeper shade of red.

The girl waved it off. "No need to be embarrassed. Like I said, your brooding is very attractive—and it was nothing like all those posers who only wanted attention. I could tell that you were for real, that something deep was going on inside of you. I used to lie in bed at night thinking if only I could hug all your troubles away and make you smile more." She laughed, not at Dylan but herself. "I was an insufferable romantic back then."

"That doesn't sound like such a bad thing."

"Well, it is when it's unrequited."

Dylan's lips parted, but nothing came out; the feeling of shame washed over him again.

"Oh no, I didn't mean it like that," the girl added quickly. "You were one of the good guys. And you never made me feel ashamed or awkward. In fact, you made me feel special. Believe it or not, those smiles from you got me through a lot of rough days."

The shame still burned inside him. Not because he didn't remember her—now that she had jogged his memory, he recalled the redheaded girl with freckles he'd caught stealing glances at him in the hallways and the cafeteria at school; she would have been fifteen at the time but looked even younger. The shame he felt now came from another memory. Shortly before graduation, he had found a note in his locker—an anonymous love note. He should have just tucked it into his pocket and read it later, but he'd opened it and started reading it right there in the hallway. Before he'd even got through the first paragraph, one of his buddies, Jayce McMullen, had torn the note out of his hands and read the entire thing out loud.

Everyone in the hallway had started oohing and aahing and clapping and laughing. Everyone, except the shy redheaded girl with the freckles. She hadn't cried and run off like girls in the movies do. She'd just stood there in the background, looking at Dylan with a sad expression. And Dylan had stood there, looking ashamed because he should have stopped Jayce from reading the note.

The lovely auburn-haired girl smiled at Dylan now.

The same smile she'd given him back in the Red Lounge—a ghostly smile that raised the fine hair on his forearms. Then, as if plucking the thoughts straight from his head, she said, "It wasn't me, you know."

Dylan froze, trying to look like he didn't know what she was talking about, but her smile only deepened.

"The love note," she said. "The one you found in your locker that day. The one that muscle-head Jayce McMullen snatched from you and read out loud in the hallway—he was a real prize, eh? I didn't write it." Her smile became sly at Dylan's confusion. "But I wish I had. It was actually pretty good."

It was silent for a moment, and then at the same time, they both laughed.

"Oh my god," she said, genuinely remorseful, "you look so embarrassed right now. I thought it would make you feel better to know the truth, and it only made you feel worse!" But she couldn't stop laughing, and Dylan couldn't stop smiling, despite his ever-reddening cheeks.

At Dylan's side, Hakhan's ears perked up, and a low sound between a whine and a growl escaped his throat. But Dylan and the girl were looking into each other's eyes, and neither of them heard the elevator ding. So when the doors slid open, they were both taken by surprise. A clipped scream came from the girl before she could stop it, and immediately she put her hand over her mouth to stifle a fresh burst of laughter. Dylan, whose body had tensed reflexively at the sudden sound of the elevator doors opening, released a soundless breath, along with a smile of embarrassment.

5

"There you are," Charlie said, stepping from the elevator. "I thought something had happened to you. I've sent like a million texts. Didn't you get any of them?"

Dylan was looking at the girl and smiling, but his heart was still thumping a little from the jolt. "My battery was running low, so I turned off my phone."

"Why didn't you just charge it in your car?"

"I couldn't find the cord—I think I might have left it here or back in New York. I'm sorry. I didn't mean to worry you."

Charlie stood a little straighter, with his chin raised. "I wasn't worried. Just concerned. You said you weren't that far away. I thought something might have happened. You have to remember to charge your phone, Dylan. It's very important. In case of emergencies. If something happened to Father or Grandmother, and I needed to get in touch with you—"

Charlie stopped abruptly as if noticing for the first time that Dylan was still looking at the girl with a very un-Dylanlike smile on his face. A boyishly bashful smile that disconcerted Charlie because it made his older brother look slightly dim. They were Latners, after all, and Latners were anything but dim.

Charlie looked at the girl and then back at Dylam and with an awkward smile asked, "Did I miss something?"

Dylan looked at his younger brother with a smile that wasn't quite so dim anymore but still distractingly uncharacteristic and shook his head. "No. Happy New Year, Charlie."

Charlie pushed out a half-smile and with a formal nod responded, "Happy New Year, Dylan." And with a nod to the girl, he said, "Happy New Year, Lexie."

"Happy New Year, Charlie," she said with a warm laugh, and she kissed him on the cheek.

Charlie took a breath, raising his slender chest. "Well, I see you two have met."

Dylan smiled at the girl and said, "Well, not officially."

Charlie pressed his lips together and with another short nod, he said, "Lexie, this is my older brother, Dylan. Dylan, this is Lexie. We go to school together—at least we used to. Lexie graduated in June, and she's now attending NYU. She's majoring in business management, just like you, Dylan—and like me . . . next fall, at least . . . after I graduate from high school. You two should have a lot to talk about." A glint of pride shone in Charlie's eyes when he added, "Dylan will be graduating from Harvard this year . . . 'this year' meaning after midnight, of course."

"Oh, Harvard," Lexie said. "Impressive."

"I was accepted to Harvard as well," Charlie interjected in the same formal manner he often adopted when in the company of anyone outside of the family circle. "Yale and MIT as well. But I'll be attending Cornell instead. So that I can stay close to home—for Father and Grandmother, mostly, but also because I don't like to travel as much as Dylan here."

Dylan winked at Lexie. "Charlie isn't a fan of flying."

Charlie bristled slightly. "I don't mind *flying*. I just don't like to do it unless it's necessary."

Dylan smiled kindly. "But he likes riding shotgun through the desert with the top down."

Charlie tried to suppress a smile. "I do enjoy a good ride."

"With the oldies turned up full volume on the radio," Dylan added, chipping further away at his brother's stiff façade.

"The music of our father's generation is certainly superior to anything coming out today," Charlie concurred with a nod that didn't seem quite so stiff this time.

Lexie said, "I love the oldies. Sia, The Lumineers, FIYM, Ed Sheeran—*Divide* is my absolute favorite—AWOLNATION, The Weeknd, Gaga, Katy Perry, Bieber—oh, my god, he's so sexy!"

Charlie snorted with a chuckle of disbelief. "Ew, Lexie. Bieber? He's like Grandmother's age!"

"No, he's not," Lexie said, laughing. "He's sixty-two. Your grandmother is thirteen years older than him."

"That's still way too old for you," Charlie said, trying not to laugh. "He's older than Father! He wasn't even born in this century! And he has all those tattoos all over his body!"

"Your brother has tattoos," Lexie countered.

Charlie's cheeks flushed at Dylan's quizzical glance; though Dylan had never kept his tattoos a secret, it was a bit surprising that Charlie had told this girl about them.

"Yes," Charlie said quickly, "but only *two*—not all over his body like some walking billboard!" Charlie shot a sudden look of alarm at Dylan and said, "Tell me you don't have any more."

Dylan shook his head with a smile. He liked seeing Charlie like this, joking with this pretty girl from school who had so effortlessly pulled the starch from his stiff collar and got him to lower his guard and just let loose like a normal teenager.

The last time Dylan had seen his younger brother was at the family Christmas gathering in New York, where the mood had been tense but civil. By their grandmother's strict decree, no one discussed politics or the recent election. Even the old man had held his tongue—a monumental occurrence which, under normal circumstances, would have given Dylan some small measure of private amusement. But the aftershock of his last encounter with Charlie—a real scorcher that had left them both feeling raw—had dulled his capacity for amusement.

That had been back in early November. Charlie had pushed him hard, and Dylan had said things that he wished he could take back, and neither of them had attempted to make contact with the other over the six weeks following the election. Not even so much as a phone call or a text.

Though they'd had their fair share of disagreements over the years—most of them about their father—Dylan had always been able to get Charlie to see reason. But something had changed over the course of the election. Charlie's tolerance for reason had plummeted while his capacity for the outlandish and mendacious claims the old man spewed at his rallies only seemed to rise and expand with each passing day.

The day before the election, Charlie had flown from New York to Boston on one of the family's three helicopters. From the airport, he'd been chauffeured in a shiny black bulletproof limousine to make a dramatic entrance at Harvard, accompanied by a detail of Secret Service agents that had been assigned to protect him shortly after the old man's victory in the Republican primaries.

Charlie had caught Dylan between classes, and things quickly got out of hand when Charlie attempted to strongarm his older brother into coming back to New York to be with the family on election night. They were outside of the Science Center, where the air was crisp and the crowd was thick.

"Maybe we should have this talk in private," Dylan had suggested in a calm tone.

"No," Charlie said, stiffening. "I think I'd rather have this chat right down here in public. So that I don't lose my composure and say something we'll both regret."

Dylan bit his tongue and forced an awkward smile that looked more like a grimace. He had tried hard to avoid discussing the election with Charlie over the past year and a half, and for the most part, he had succeeded. But Charlie was pushing with such force now that it was difficult not to push back.

"Father is a great man," Charlie said. "A visionary leader who will bring greatness back to our country. He can do it, Dylan. I've seen it. And if you'd just watch his speeches, if you'd just look at the crowds, the energy—it's electrifying, hauntingly similar to Great-grandfather. Why can't you see this?"

"I have seen it," Dylan said. "And you're right. It's hauntingly similar to our great-grandfather."

Charlie smiled with a sigh of relief. "Then surely you—"

"Dad's Crazy, Charlie." It came out like a slap to the face, and though it hurt Dylan to see the wounded look in his brother's eyes, he couldn't stop the words from tumbling out. "He's as crazy as our great-grandfather was—and a lot more dangerous because he's better at hiding just how crazy he is. The things he's been saying, the wild rhetoric, the blatant lies, the shitstorm he's stirring up to divide us—that's just the beginning. It's going to get worse. A lot worse."

Charlie stood in stunned disbelief for a moment. Then he shook his head sadly, but there was a hard, unforgiving sheen in his eyes. "You know, Dylan, I look at you and sometimes wonder how you could possibly be Father's son."

"Yeah, me too," Dylan said softly.

"We *are* his sons, you and I, and that makes us better."

"Better than who?"

"Everyone."

Dylan's lips parted, but Charlie cut him off.

"Father has afforded us protection from public scrutiny. He has sheltered us from the vicious attacks of the false media. They want to devour him, Dylan. They want to tear his pure soul apart and destroy all that he loves. He is an honorable man, and it is our responsibility to honor and obey him."

They stood there in the cold, bright daylight, each gazing into the other's eyes, neither willing to back down.

Then Dylan said softly, "You don't know him. You don't know what he's capable of, all the things that he's done, the lives that he's destroyed to get where he is."

Charlie laughed, mirthlessly. "I didn't know you were so prone to dramatics, Dylan. You were always so stoic. 'The lives he's destroyed'—really? And *you* accuse *him* of hyperbole?"

Dylan didn't take the bait.

Charlie sighed, and his features suddenly softened. "You need to be with the family tomorrow night. We need to show our solidarity. We can go to the polls together, let the country see that we are united, that we stand together for them. So much is hanging in the balance here. The future of the country—the right direction. Surely you can see this. You can't not see this, Dylan. We are on the precipice. Father is our only hope. People see you—*young* people—they look up to you. They trust you. Did you see the numbers at FiveThirtyEight? You poll higher with the eighteen to thirty-five demographic than either Father or Caitlyn Price! They loved the way you stood up to Father at the Fastball College Tour event!"

Dylan remained silent. Charlie's eyes darkened momentarily and then brightened.

"At first, I was angry with you—and Father was absolutely livid—but then I realized the genius of it. By standing up to Father in front of all those college kids on national TV, you'd asserted your *independence*. You'd made your judgment *unimpeachable*. They trust you because you didn't just jump on and throw your support to Father because you're his son. You made him *work* for your vote!"

Dylan held his tongue as well as his gaze, waiting for Charlie to finish.

"It was brilliant, Dylan," Charlie beamed. "You hooked them all, and now tomorrow morning when they see you go to the polls with the family, they'll see that Father earned your vote! You don't even have to say anything. Just smile for the camera after you cast your ballot. The younger voters will see you there, and they'll follow suit. Because you're a leader, Dylan, and they want to be led because they're like sheep. They'll follow you, trust me. All you have to do is *lead* them."

Dylan gazed at Charlie in silence. The hope in his younger brother's eyes brought on a seemingly insurmountable wave of emotion, but Dylan pushed back against it. He would do anything for Charlie. Anything but this one thing. It was the line in the sand that he could not bring himself to cross. Even for the person he loved more than anyone else on earth, he could not bring himself to do it.

The shift in Charlie's features happened gradually, as if in phases of stop-motion, until his cheeks were red and his lips pressed into a thin, bloodless line. It took him a while to find his voice, but when he did, the words came tumbling out like poison.

"You've always hated Father. As far back as I can remember, you've opposed him at every turn. You never even gave him a chance. You just hated him without cause, without justification. Even when you were little. So hateful, chipping away at his soul, glaring at him with such contempt, and I don't know why. I don't know what could possibly make a son—who owes his very life to his father—treat that father with such disrespect, such blatant scorn. Spiteful, nasty, cruel . . . "

Charlie shook his head. Dylan remained silent. Neither of them broke eye contact.

"This one time," Charlie went on, "this one time that he needs you, more than anything, and you won't throw him so much as a bone? You won't step down from that high horse and stand with him when he needs you more than anything? You won't stand by him even when the future of your country is at stake? You're not worried about *that?*"

This time Dylan did speak. "That's exactly what I'm worried about, Charlie."

Charlie snorted an ironic laugh. "Then why won't you stand by him?" He looked deeply into Dylan's eyes and saw something that both frightened and enraged him at once, and with a look of indignation and incredulous disbelief, he spat, "You're not with *her*, are you, Dylan?"

"I'm not with anybody."

But Charlie didn't believe him. "God, I wish I had your vote," he seethed with disgust. "I wish I could steal your vote, I swear it. People like you shouldn't be allowed to cast a ballot in a free and fair election."

"That would sort of defeat the purpose of the free and fair part, wouldn't it?"

"Don't be such a smartass, Dylan. It's very unbecoming."

"Don't be such a blind follower, Charlie. It'll come back to bite you in the ass. Just ask all those Kool-Aid drinkers who followed our great-grandfather off the cliff."

Charlie was stunned into momentary silence. Then he found his center and lashed out with the only weapon that he was certain would draw blood.

With a chilly smirk, he said, "Is this about my mother? Are you still obsessing over that? She was disturbed, mentally and emotionally disturbed. What she did to herself had nothing to do with Father. You can't pin that on him." He probed Dylan's eyes and then snorted an incredulous laugh. "What? Are you suggesting that Father *killed* her and made it look like a suicide? That's rich! That's dramatic! You might want to seriously consider therapy, Dylan, if that's what you're thinking."

Again, Dylan didn't take the bait.

Charlie laughed bitterly. "Come on, Dylan, tell me all about it. Tell me what Father did to my mother. Tell me how he drove her to open her own wrists in the bathtub. Tell me how anybody can be responsible for someone doing something like that to herself. Tell me all about it. Tell me what horrible, unspeakable, vile thing Father did to my mother. I'm all ears."

Dylan stood still for a moment, trying to push back against the impulse, trying to remind himself that Charlie was just a kid, almost but not yet seventeen, and that there were things he could not accept about their father, their lives, their family—not just yet, anyway.

He waited for the moment to pass, for the burn to cool, and he almost succeeded in suppressing the fire within.

But then Charlie did something.

He rolled his eyes and shook his head with a condescending smile. And for a brief second, he looked just like the old man. And that was enough to send Dylan over the edge.

"You want to know what Dad did to your mother, Charlie?" he said in an oddly calm tone. "He raped her."

Charlie shook his head with pursed lips. "A husband cannot rape his wife, Dylan. It is a wife's duty to see to her husband's needs."

Dylan froze, his jaw tensing, his nostrils flaring. Then he shook his head in stupefied wonder, and said, "Do you hear yourself, Charlie? Do you hear how crazy that sounds?"

Charlie's features hardened, and his eyes glazed over icily. "I'm not crazy," he said, his hands clenching into fists at his sides.

"I'm not saying *you're* crazy, Charlie. I'm saying that what you *said* is crazy." He searched his brother's eyes for a sign that he was getting through. Then he spoke succinctly. "He raped her, Charlie. He grabbed your mother by the pussy—his words, not mine—and he forced himself on her. That's real news. Not fake. It's fact. It happened. Do you get that?"

Charlie raised his chin and with stiff lips said, "The charges were dropped. She recanted everything. It was all a lie. The media loves to use Father as a punching bag; they'll say anything—"

"He beat her, Charlie," Dylan said flatly. "We both saw the bruises on her face and neck. He punched your mother and strangled her while he raped her."

Charlie was trembling now, but he steeled his body and said, "She dropped the charges." Then he gave a curt nod as if to say the matter was closed. But Dylan wasn't finished.

"She dropped the charges because she was terrified of him—"

"She dropped the charges," Charlie interjected, "because they were—" He almost said "fake" but instead said, "—false. Completely erroneous and false. Made up to hurt Father because he'd scorned her with another woman. She was jealous."

Dylan stared at his brother for a moment and then laughed a humorless laugh, short and soundless. "Are you kidding me? You're mother wanted nothing to do with him. She wanted to take both of us and leave. That night. Maybe you were too young to remember—you were like six at the time—but I was older, and I do remember. I was standing outside of their room when she told him that she wanted to take you and me and leave. I saw him, Charlie. I saw the look in his eyes, and it was like nothing you've ever seen."

Charlie stood frozen, unable to tear his eyes away from his older brother's gaze. He wanted Dylan to stop talking about it, but he couldn't make his tongue work. He swallowed nervously, waiting for the hammer to fall, and in seconds, it did.

"And then he hit her, Charlie," Dylan said. "Not like a slap. He hit her the way a guy would hit another guy. Not with an open hand. With a fist. She didn't fly backwards like in the movies. She staggered and dropped to her knees. There was blood coming from her nose and her mouth, but I don't think she knew it. I don't think she knew much of anything—at least not until he started tearing her clothes off."

Dylan paused. Tears stood in his eyes, but they didn't fall. Charlie wanted to look away, but he couldn't. He just stared into Dylan's eyes, wishing he would stop talking and just come back to New York to be with the family on election night.

"He saw me," Dylan said. "Standing there in the doorway. He saw me looking at her, sitting on the floor and bleeding. And he came to the door and looked down at me—and I swear to you, Charlie, if I'd had a knife or a gun, I would have killed him."

Charlie shuddered but quickly recovered and stiffened his chin defiantly. "Now who sounds crazy, Dylan? Do you hear yourself? If you'd had a knife or a gun, you would have killed Father? Do you know how crazy that sounds?"

But Dylan wasn't about to let his kid brother turn it around on him. Not this time.

"And do you know what he said to me, Charlie? He said, 'Your mother isn't feeling well. Go find your little brother an play with him.'" Tears threatened again, but Dylan held them back. "And then he closed the door and locked it."

Charlie stood frozen. The pulse pounded at Dylan's temples, but he forced himself to go on because this was something Charlie needed to hear.

"And then he raped her, Charlie. While I stood outside in the hallway, he raped her. I could hear him tearing her clothes off, and I could hear her crying out for him to stop, please stop, and I just stood there frozen. I didn't run for help. I didn't pound on the door. I just stood there, like I was out of my body, floating. But I could hear it. I could hear everything, and I just stood there. There was a monster in the house, and he was hurting Mom, and I just stood there. I was ten years old."

Time seemed to stand still as the two brothers fell into a long silence, their warm breath hitting the cold air in white plumes while nearby Charlie's Secret Service detail stood like statues in their dark overcoats and sunglasses.

It was Charlie who broke the silence when he asked, "Do you know what it's like to be raped, Dylan? Have you ever been raped?"

Dylan's lips parted, but nothing came out. The casual tone of Charlie's voice had cut him to the core. And when he looked into Charlie's eyes, he saw nothing even remotely resembling human compassion.

"I only ask," Charlie continued in that same casual tone, "because if you haven't ever been raped, how could you know whether what you heard was truly a rape?"

The discussion had ended there. Dylan had simply turned and walked away, leaving Charlie with his Secret Service detail on the cold stone walkway in front of the Science Center.

He hadn't joined the family on the night of the election. Instead, he'd stayed in Cambridge and watched the returns on TV in his dorm room. The pundits had dubbed it the "Rematch of the Century"—Caitlyn Price, the granddaughter of Hannah Crichton, versus Jake Latner, the grandson of Royal Kingley—and posed the questions: "Will lightning strike twice?" "Can Latner pull off an electoral victory over Price like his grandfather managed over Hannah forty years ago on this very night?" "Will we see another shocking split between the popular vote and the electoral college or will the country unify for a solid victory one way or the other?" "Does Latner have enough of the old Kingley chutz-pah to sweep the swing states and steal one of Crichton's blue states out from under her to clinch the prize?" "Are we in for an all-night, edge-of-our-seats nail-biter or a sudden-death blowout?"

It had not only ended up being the latter; it had been a brutal trouncing.

By nine P.M., EST—two hours before the California polls had even closed—every news outlet, including FIX, had called the race for Caitlyn Price. And by the following morning, her victory in the electoral college stood at 433 to 104, and in the popular vote, a staggering margin of 27.19 percent.

6

Charlie snapped his fingers twice in front of Dylan's eyes and said, "Earth to Dylan, come in, Dylan."

Dylan blinked, coming out of the memory, and Charlie laughed, a genuine laugh that made Dylan smile, which in turn made Lexie smile.

"Just the two," Charlie said, "Right?"

"The two what?"

"*Tattoos,*" Charlie said, laughing harder. "You just have the two, right? You didn't get any more of them, did you?"

Dylan nodded, remembering his place in the conversation. "No, I didn't get any more."

"Swear it," Charlie said, still laughing.

"I swear it," Dylan said, crossing his heart. "Just the two."

He was relieved to see that Charlie had gotten over their dustup at Harvard, but it was a tentative sort of relief. Often with Charlie, what showed up on the surface merely masked the real turmoil within. Back in second grade, Charlie had been sent home for "conduct unbecoming a Carrington

Academy student." After a boy had accidentally smeared his painting in first-period art class, Charlie not only accepted the boy's apology with a pleasant smile but waited half the day to exact his revenge. At lunch, Charlie entered the cafeteria, approached the boy from behind at a casual gate, and dumped a jar of red paint over the boy's head.

Dylan hadn't been in the cafeteria at the time of the incident, but he'd been called down to the office to sit with Charlie until their mother arrived. When he'd asked Charlie why he had dumped the paint on the boy after the boy had already apologized for smearing the painting, Charlie looked him in the eye and responded calmly, "He wasn't really sorry, Dylan. He just said that he was sorry so he wouldn't get punished. Now he knows that his actions have consequences."

Dylan was still picturing his seven-year-old brother on that day in the principal's office—that eerily solemn look in his eyes—when Lexie pulled him back to the present with a sly grin and a teasing chuckle. "Now you've got me curious about these tattoos. Are they private or public?"

Dylan laughed in spite of himself, and Hakhan, who had been sitting dutifully at his side, suddenly jumped up and planted his front paws on Dylan's shoulders again.

As the large dog pelted Dylan's face with kisses, Charlie flinched—a scarcely noticeable gesture—and made a sour face. He recovered quickly and pushed out a fairly convincing smile. "I see someone got out again," he said in a tight yet pleasant tone. "I'll have to have a word with Jaime."

With his huge head resting on Dylan's shoulder, Hakhan looked demurely at Charlie before turning back to Dylan and giving him another kiss.

"You wouldn't know it by looking at him," Charlie said to Lexie, "but Hakhan hails from a long line of championship Alsatian Shepalutes, descendants of the extinct Dire wolf. Brave guardians and skillful hunters. Grandmother brought this one's great-great-grandfather over from France when Father was still a boy—they have a remarkably long life span for a large breed—and we've had them in the family ever since. Father loathes animals, especially dogs, but Grandmother still signs the checks." He allowed a thin smile, which vanished the moment his eyes fell on the dog fawning over Dylan. "We have three others from Hakhan's litter—all excellent guard dogs and very obedient. But, as you can see, Dylan spoiled this one, and now he's practically useless for his purpose."

"You're not useless," Dylan cooed to the dog. "You just haven't decided what your purpose is yet."

"Eating, sleeping, running aimlessly around the grounds, and getting into all manner of mischief," Charlie said with a short eye-roll.

"That doesn't sound like such a bad life," Dylan said, smiling at Hakhan and stroking his furry cheeks. "You're a free spirit, aren't you."

"Without any restraint or rules," Charlie snorted. "See how far that gets you."

"I thought you were a free-market regulation-buster like Dad," Dylan said with a wink.

Charlie's gaze turned stormy for a brief second, and then he smiled. "Dogs aren't people, Dylan."

"And people aren't dogs, Charlie."

Charlie had almost forgotten how smoothly Dylan could deliver a stinging comeback, the sort that scarcely left a scar. The last thing he wanted right now was to get into another argument, but the retort was out of his mouth before he could stop it. "Unbridled obstinacy isn't a virtue. You've made him uneducable."

"Is that really a word?" Dylan asked with a skeptical smile, his tone bordering on condescension.

"Yes, Dylan," Charlie said, working to keep his own tone civil, "it *is* a word. It means incapable of being educated.

Incapable of learning even basic commands that the average mongrel could master with ease, like sitting and staying or even rolling over and playing dead."

"You mean like tricks?"

Charlie's eyes iced over slightly, but his smile remained in place. "Yes, like 'tricks.'"

"He knows tricks," Dylan said, and he looked into Hakhan's eyes. "Hakhan, where's the striker?" The dog gave him a curious look because Dylan had never asked this particular question indoors before. But his ears stood fully upright. "Center field, go get him."

In a flash, Hakhan leapt back and bolted halfway down the hall, where he turned fast and faced Dylan in a rigid stance. The expectant look in his eyes was the same as it had been outside on the east lawn, where Dylan use to practice spot-kicks while Hakhan guarded the goal. The huge dog was a better goalkeeper than any Dylan had ever faced on the pitch in a real game—so good, in fact, that every now and again Dylan employed a crafty tactic to get around his superior defense. He would call out "Incoming," and Hakhan would immediately drop down onto his belly and cover his snout with his forepaws just in time for the ball to sail over him and into the net at the end of the field.

It wasn't a command that Hakhan had been taught. It was just something he'd picked up through observation when he was a puppy. There was an old war movie playing on TV one afternoon while Hakhan was patiently waiting for Dylan to finish his homework. The near constant explosion of bombs and fireworks on-screen had grabbed the pup's attention and held it. But it wasn't until Dylan had closed his books that he noticed what was going on. Every time a soldier in the movie called out "Incoming," Hakhan would drop down and cover his head along with the other soldiers on-screen.

Now as the dog stood halfway down the hall, his gaze fixed on Dylan, his body poised for action, Dylan called out, "Incoming," and without hesitation, Hakhan dropped down and covered his snout. He waited a few extra seconds for the sound of the whizzing ball overhead; when it didn't come, he sprang to his feet and raced to the far end of the hall. He was still sniffing around for the ball when Charlie chimed in cynically, "Impressive trick."

Dylan shrugged with a sheepish grin. "Well, there's supposed to be a ball there."

Lexie purred, "Awwwwww, he's adorable."

Charlie rolled his eyes. Dylan clicked his tongue, and Hakhan came running back to him.

"I'll call one of the handlers to take him back to the kennels," Charlie said, knowing what Dylan's response would be.

"Nah, let him out for a while," Dylan said, petting Hakhan. "He's a big guy, he needs to stretch his legs. Don't you, buddy? That's right, Hakhan is a very big boy."

Charlie raised his chin. "You'll have to be responsible for him—"

"I will."

"You know how he gets—"

"I know. He'll be fine."

"Especially around Akasha. He incites her."

"Who's Akasha?" Lexie asked.

Charlie gave her an odd look. His lips parted, but Dylan beat him to the punch.

"Morgana's cat," he said.

"Morgana's prized Norwegian Forest cat," Charlie added for clarification. "Very large, very exotic-looking domestic breed with sharp eyes and sharper claws. Dylan is the only one who can get near her—aside from Morgana, of course. She tolerates the rest of us—just barely—except for Father. The two of them have been at odds ever since Akasha scratched him—do you remember that, Dylan?"

"How could I forget?" Dylan said with a half smile.

"Well," Charlie said, "I suppose it's a little funny now,

but it was pretty serious at the time. Father almost needed stitches—"

Dylan laughed. "It was just a scratch, Charlie."

"There was a great deal of blood if you recall," Charlie countered. "The tablecloth had to be pitched. Lupita tried, but she just couldn't get out all the blood."

"Oh my god," Lexie said with a half-smile of shock. "What happened?"

Charlie's cheeks flared crimson, not with anger but embarrassment. "Dylan and I were messing about at the dinner table—just spirited good-natured fun, the sort boys do. I had started it by catapulting one of my brussels sprouts with a spoon across the table at Dylan, and he returned fire. Father became irritated—understandably so; he'd had a long day at work and didn't like horseplay at the table. He turned to Dylan and started dressing him down. I suppose nothing would have come of it—nothing often does when Father goes off on one of his rants. But when he slammed the table and pointed his finger at Dylan, things . . . escalated."

Lexie's brow furrowed.

Charlie flushed again, and with a weak smile elaborated, "Akasha suddenly sprang out of nowhere, landed on the table between Father and Dylan, and lashed out at Father."

"Holy shit!" Lexie said with wide eyes as she tried to stifle a laugh.

"Like I said," Charlie went on with a nod. "It seems funny in retrospect, but it was quite serious at the time. I truly thought Father was going to strike Akasha, possibly even stab her with his knife—in self-defense, of course. But I think he was afraid of her. She didn't run after clawing him. She just stood there on the table with her ears back and this spooky growl rising in her throat—do you remember it, Dylan?"

Dylan nodded. But this time, he wasn't smiling. He remembered the scene with perfect clarity. The large cat had held her ground, effectively blocking the old man from getting to Dylan. Her fur stood in hackles and her back was arched as if she was gearing up for another attack at any sign of movement from the old man. Dylan had seen dogs poised to strike like this in defense of their masters, but he had never seen a cat do it, even a large cat like Akasha.

"Anyway," Charlie continued, "Father was terribly angry. You could hear him shouting from the kitchen as Lupita held his hand under the faucet—all sorts of obscenities—do you remember it, Dylan?"

Dylan remembered. The old man had gone off like a wildfire in high wind, scorching everything in its path.

"That fuckin cat is gone! I want that bitch euthanized! You see what she did to me? That dirty bitch! I'll cut her fuckin tail off and feed it to her! Looked me dead in the eye—dead in the fuckin eye, like *she* pays the fuckin bills around here, like *she's* the master of the house! I'll show her who's the master! She wants a war, she's got one, let me tell you, fuckin hairy devil she-bitch!"

Then he was shouting toward the dining room, "She's fuckin dead, Morgana! Do you hear me? You're fucking precious little she-bitch from Norway that cost me two grand—" (Aside to Lupita, he muttered, "Can you fucking believe that? Two grand! Unbelievable! The dirty little traitor bitch!") "—she's dead, Morgana. I swear to you on every fuckin thing that I hold sacred, that miserable fucking filthy ball of fur—disgusting, really—she's dead! I'm gonna kill her, I'm gonna gut her, and I'm gonna stuff her, just you wait and see—that miserable, evil, mangy, ungrateful fucking she-bitch, biting the hand that feeds her—she's dead! D-E-A-D, dead! Say goodbye to your vile little foo-foo feline free-loader, Morgana, because I'm gonna rip every one of those fucking claws out of her dainty little paws that have to have fresh litter on a daily fuckin basis—fresh litter, like she's too good to shit in day-old litter, can you believe that happy shit? You don't bite the hand that feeds you! You don't *ever* do that! She's dead—boy, is she ever dead, that dirty dirty *dirty* slinking little bitch . . . "

Dylan could still see Morgana sitting at the end of the table, calmly sipping her wine as if dinner had never been interrupted.

"Father wasn't able to convince Morgana to get rid of Akasha, of course," Charlie said to Lexie. "But he banned her from the New York residence, and so she lives down here year round." He dropped a wink. "Morgana spends more time down here anyway. And when Father does come down for a weekend, he and Akasha have an understanding and mostly avoid one another."

"I can see why," Lexie said with a chuckle. "Still, she sounds like an interesting cat. I hope I get to meet her."

"Oh, I'm sure she's around here someplace," Charlie said in a sing-song tone. "She'll most likely come out now that Dylan's here. Like I said, outside of Morgana, he's her favorite."

Lexie nudged Dylan. "You never told me you had a badass guardian cat."

"You never asked," he said with a smile.

"So," Lexie said, clapping her hands together, "who's going to give me the tour of this place?"

Before Dylan could speak, Charlie said, "Dylan can show you around. I'm sure there's a lot of people here he hasn't got the chance to catch up with, and you can introduce him to the people he doesn't know."

"That sounds like a plan to me," Lexie said.

Still petting Hakhan behind his ear, Dylan looked at Charlie and opened his mouth to speak, but again Charlie beat him to the punch.

"We'll have plenty of time to have that talk later. It's New Year's Eve. You have to celebrate a little. And Lexie needs a tour guide. This is her first visit, and she'll get lost wandering around alone. I'd do it myself, but I'm working on the preparations for the midnight finale."

Dylan's eyes narrowed. "What's the 'midnight finale?'"

Charlie smiled. "It's a surprise. I've been working on it all month."

"Well, what's the surprise?"

"You'll just have to stick around to find out with the rest of the guests."

Dylan couldn't help responding to Charlie with a smile of his own, albeit a curious one. "Yeah, but I'm not one of the guests. I'm family."

"Tonight," Charlie said with a wink and a nod, "everyone is a guest. So just relax and unwind. At midnight, all will be revealed. I promise, you'll like it—or at least you'll appreciate all the work I put into it."

Dylan had the tentative look in his eyes that usually gave Charlie hope because it meant that he was on the bubble, and when Dylan was on the bubble about anything, he almost always came down on the side of his heart.

Charlie worked up his courage and gave it a gentle nudge. "It's for you," he said, "the surprise. I made it for you. For all that you've done. You probably won't love it—I know that—but you'll appreciate it. And I worked the whole month on it."

The hopeful look in Charlie's eyes tipped the scales, and Dylan nodded. He could stay for the surprise, have his talk with Charlie, and then quietly leave. "Just till midnight, right?"

"Just till midnight, I swear."

"All right, I'll stick around."

"Perfect!" Charlie beamed. "Now, you two go and enjoy the party. I've got a ton of things to attend to—I've worked very hard on this thing, and I don't want any hiccups. Timing is crucial, and everything needs to go off without a hitch, or it could be a disaster, and nobody wants that, trust me."

Dylan could hardly believe the change in Charlie's demeanor since they'd last seen each other at Christmas in

New York. The kid was practically trembling with excitement. Dylan hadn't seen his younger brother this elated in years, and he couldn't help but smile at such delight.

"All right then," Charlie said with a grin, clapping his hands together. The sudden sound made Hakhan shrink back against Dylan's leg, but Dylan didn't notice. He was too focused on his brother's happiness. "We'll meet up in the Atrium before midnight—say eleven thirty—and have that private talk. That should give us more than enough time before the surprise. Yes?"

Dylan nodded. "Sure."

Lexie smiled with narrowed eyes. "Private talks, midnight surprises—should I be feeling left out here?"

She was only teasing, but Charlie's response came with utter sincerity. "Oh, no, not at all. You're going to have a front row seat so you don't miss a thing."

They looked at one another, Lexie and Charlie, and then they both broke into laughter, the sort of spontaneous laughter that good friends often do for no reason at all.

Still laughing, Lexie said, "You're up to something—you have that sneaky look. This better not be something that's gonna scare me!"

"You'll just have to wait and see," Charlie said with a grin as he backed away.

"I'm serious, Charlie," Lexie called after him.

Charlie called back, "You're gonna love it." And to Dylan, he added, "Remember to keep an eye on Hakhan, especially around Akasha. Don't let him challenge her. Her nails haven't been clipped since last month, and Father will have a fit if there's blood all over the carpets."

7

The activity in the Red Lounge had tamed considerably by the time Dylan and Lexie returned from their tour of the ground floor residence.

They took the corner sofa opposite the glass wall, whose sliding panels opened onto the patio outside. Most of the guests were out there enjoying the pool, and to Dylan's surprise, no one was naked. Even with the drinks flowing and the music blasting from the speakers, the guests, all of them between Dylan's and Charlie's ages, appeared to be adhering to Charlie's rules of propriety. Of course, it was still pretty early, and Dylan could not imagine a scenario in which at least one couple at this party didn't find their way to one of the rooms upstairs.

Lexie sipped her beer while, beside her, Dylan watched the celebration out on the patio with a glint of nostalgia in his eyes. The muted sounds coming from the opposite side of the long glass wall played in his ears more like a memory than background noise at a New Year's bash hosted by his kid brother.

I'm working on preparations for the midnight finale . . . it's a surprise.

Not so long ago, it had been Charlie standing on that diving board and Dylan waiting in the water, telling him that he could do it, assuring him that it was perfectly safe. Then the two of them racing the length of the pool, splashing and diving and competing to see who could hold his breath longer under water. All those warm summer evenings and hot sunny days that seemed like they would never end, back when the sound of Charlie's laughter was the only thing Dylan needed to make him smile. But suddenly, that seemed like a lifetime ago. Something had changed between then and now, and Dylan wasn't sure if he would ever be able to get that happy feeling back.

"Do you want to go for a dip?"

Dylan shook his head with a small smile.

"I'll do it," Lexie said. "Dare me, and I'll go out there and strip and dive in right now."

Dylan's eyes widened.

"Of course," she added, blushing slightly, "you'll have to join me—I'm not brave enough to do it on my own."

For an odd second, he thought she was serious. And for an even odder second, he found himself considering the proposal. Then Lexie broke into a shocked grin and put a hand to her mouth.

"Oh my god, you were actually considering it!"

"I wasn't," he said with reddening cheeks.

"You were!" she squealed softly and shook her head. "Damn! And I was *that* close to seeing those tattoos."

Dylan laughed.

Lexie shrugged. "Oh well, the night is still young. I'll bet I can get you to show them to me before midnight."

Dylan raised a brow and said, "You want to see them? I'll show them to you now."

Lexie smiled slyly. "Now where's the fun in that?"

He gave her a quizzical look, but she could tell that he was enjoying the game.

"You can't just roll over and give in," she said. "You have to make me *work* for it."

Dylan pondered for a second and then said simply, "OK, you had your chance."

Lexie's features froze. "Wait, are you serious? You're not going to show them to me?"

"One time only offer. You passed. Your loss."

A slow grin spread across Lexie's mouth, and she nodded. "Oh, you're good at this."

"You'll see," Dylan said, sipping his beer casually and scarcely containing a grin. "Or, more accurately, you won't."

Lexie sipped her beer and responded just as casually, "Oh, I *will* see. Just you wait and—"

She halted in mid-sentence, her body jolting so abruptly that she almost spilled her beer on Hakhan whose head was resting comfortably on her lap.

"Holy shit!" she exclaimed in a stunned half-whisper.

The large cat had sprung seemingly from nowhere and landed gracefully on the back of the sofa. She stood there for a brief moment, her amber eyes gleaming under the dim lights of the Red Lounge. Then she stepped forward and placed her front paws on Dylan's left shoulder.

Hakhan looked up but did not raise his head from Lexie's lap. When the cat looked down at him, Hakhan, who had learned from painful experience the limits of feline patience (as well as the length of feline claws), blinked demurely while his long bushy tail thumped the sofa in a gesture of amity.

Dylan grinned as the cat moved in closer and sniffed at his ear. When she angled her head and began to nuzzle his cheek, he laughed and said, "Who's that? Who's manufacturing purrs in my ear?"

The cat purred louder and nuzzled deeper until Dylan

reached up and petted her. "This, if you haven't guessed it already, is Akasha," he said to Lexie.

"The famous Akasha," Lexie said with a gleam of approval in her eyes. "The one who took a piece of the mighty Jake Latner and lived to tell about it."

"I'm surprised Charlie let that one slip," Dylan said with a curious smile. "He usually guards the family secrets jealously. He must really trust you."

"He trusts me with all of his secrets," Lexie said with a sly twinkle in her eyes. "I was his go-to confidant in school—how do you think I found out about your tattoos?"

"Are we back to those already?"

"Depends. Are you gonna show me them?"

"Not a chance."

Lexie's eyes narrowed. Dylan laughed.

"I thought you wanted me to make you work for it."

"Now you're getting it," she said with a smooth grin. With a look at Akasha, she asked, "Will she let me pet her?"

Dylan turned his head and looked into Akasha's eyes. The cat touched her nose to Dylan's and then brushed her cheek against his again.

"She doesn't appear to be in attack mode," he said, "so I guess it's worth a try. Just don't go at her straight on. Come from behind."

"Are you sure? She won't think it's a sneak attack?"

"Pretty sure," Dylan said, raising his chin as Akasha nuzzled his neck.

Lexie reached out with a cautious hand.

"Don't be tentative," Dylan warned. "She can sense fear. But don't be too aggressive, either."

"You're just making that up," Lexie said with a nervous laugh.

"Maybe," Dylan said with a small smile. "Is it working?"

"Yes, so stop it," Lexie laughed. "If I get scratched, I'm blaming you."

"You're not going to get scratched—but do it quickly while she's still looking at me."

"Stop it," she said, laughing nervously. "You're scaring the shit out of me."

"Just pet her already."

"I am. You stay out of it . . ." Her hand was shaking, even as she continued to smile. Then her fingers were moving through the luxurious coat of fur, and Akasha was purring louder as she arched her back and nuzzled Dylan's neck. "Her fur is so silky."

Hakhan, who always got a little antsy when anyone else was getting attention, emitted a soft, plaintive whine through his nose, and Akasha responded with a low growl deep in her throat as she continued to nuzzle Dylan. Lexie was startled, but she didn't retract her hand.

"Hey," Dylan admonished the cat gently, "no fighting. Do you hear me?"

Akasha raised her head, looked him in the eye, and blinked languidly. Then after one last nudge of her head under his chin, she climbed down and curled up on the sofa between Dylan and Lexie, with her back to Hakhan. Her tail twitched once, and then she closed her eyes.

Lexie looked at Dylan with a furrowed brow and a curious smile. "Is she sleeping?"

"She will be. Right now she's just letting me know who's the boss." He stroked Akasha's fur, and her tail twitched again. "She's stubborn."

"She's your protector. She knows you're her boy, and she wants to make sure everyone else knows it too."

Dylan didn't respond. He just looked at Lexie with an unreadable expression.

"She loves you," Lexie said. "Animals can sense who we are, and they know you're the good guy."

Dylan's cheeks flushed.

"It's true," Lexie said. "Everyone knew it at school. Even the ones who didn't like your dad—and there were many.

But they never blamed you. They looked up to you because they could see that you were one of the good guys. You had everything anyone could possibly want—the wealth, the looks, the brand name—"

Dylan smiled curiously. "The brand name?"

"Don't laugh, it's true. You think because your father wasn't loved by everyone that his name didn't carry any weight?"

"I didn't say that."

"But you think it."

Dylan shrugged.

Lexie pressed on. "You're the great-grandson of a president. Your father was a two-term governor—a fairly successful one."

Dylan rolled his eyes.

"Some people considered him successful," Lexie said.

"Rich people considered him successful."

"True, but he did convince enough regular people to vote for him twice."

"Until they caught on and gave him the boot."

"'Gave him the boot?' What century are you from?"

Dylan laughed.

"And anyway, they didn't vote him out. He chose not to run for re-election."

"Because he knew he couldn't squeeze another term out of them. His own paper had him down by double digits."

"Also true," Lexie said with an arched brow. "But that's not the point. The point I was trying to make is, you're not like him at all. You're one of the good guys. A *real* good guy, and everyone at school could see it—don't laugh."

"I'm not laughing."

"You're laughing on the inside. I can sense it."

Dylan scrunched his eyes and tried not to smile. "You can see inside of me?"

"Yes, I can. Does that scare you?"

This time Dylan couldn't keep from smiling. "It kind of creeps me out. But in a good way," he added hastily.

"You think I'm joking."

Dylan shook his head. "I know you're serious."

They looked at one another for a moment.

"All right," Lexie said thoughtfully. "I'll give you an example."

"I'm all ears."

"Don't be smartassy. That's my job."

Dylan conceded the point with a nod and a smile. He could have spent the entire night looking into her lovely eyes. "I'm listening," he said.

Lexie thought for a moment and then said, "Back in your senior year, you went to a party at Mark Jablonski's house. There was a poker game going on downstairs—"

"It wasn't really downstairs," Dylan interjected. "It was on the ground level. A walkout basement."

"It was an *English* basement."

"Still, it was ground level."

"Whatever—I'm telling this story. Are you gonna let me tell it?"

Dylan smiled that small smile she found so irresistible. "I'm sorry. Continue."

"You were *downstairs* at the poker table," Lexie went on. "You weren't like the other guys, playing every hand. You folded a lot, and when you did go in, you won more than you lost."

Dylan nodded. It was true; he was a tight player with a keen eye, and he had the patience of a cat.

"It was pretty much a friendly game," Lexie continued. "But things took a turn when Mark started bullying the other players with his big stack. He was being particularly mean to this one kid, Rey Peralta—do you remember him?"

Dylan nodded. He remembered Rey. He was a skinny sophomore from a working-class family who, unlike most of the students at Overland Prep, had earned his way into the posh high school with a full academic scholarship. And he worked every evening at his father's restaurant in the city, busing tables and washing dishes. The last Dylan had heard, Rey had received a scholarship to Yale Law, while Mark Jablonski had gone straight from the Whartan School of Finance to an executive level position at his old man's investment firm.

"Anyway," Lexie continued, "despite Mark's bullying, Rey had built up a nice stack—a little over eighteen hundred, which wasn't bad, considering that the buy-in was only two hundred. He probably should have just quit while he was ahead, but you know what kind of family he comes from, and that was a lot of money for him."

Dylan didn't say anything, but something about the phrasing of her statement bothered him.

Lexie must have noticed this because she immediately shook her head with a mortified expression and said, "I didn't mean it that way. Oh, my god, I would never say anything against Rey's family! His parents were very good people—we used to eat at their restaurant all the time. I just meant that they didn't have the kind of money the Jablonski's do."

Dylan gave a reassuring nod to let her know that he wasn't judging her.

"Anyway, Mark kept re-raising large every time Rey raised preflop, and Rey kept folding. Right up until he didn't.

"It came down to three players: Mark, Rey, and you. Rey was under the gun, Mark was on the cutoff, and you were on the button. The blinds were twenty-five and fifty. Rey had a good hand and raised two hundred. Mark called and re-raised another two hundred, thinking he'd take it right there. But then you surprised everybody—especially Mark—by calling. You'd been playing so tight all night, they assumed you must have had something fairly strong to call that large of a bet from the player under the gun, not to mention the re-raise from the cutoff.

"Rey thought about it and then called Mark's three-bet too. By that point, everyone else had folded." Her eyes suddenly sparkled. "Then the flop came out: Ace-Three-Five, Club-Diamond-Spade rainbow. Rey waited for a second and then checked. Mark wanted to bet, but he was worried that you had the Ace, so he checked too. Then you just sat there with this unreadable look on your face, and everyone was like holding their breath. And then finally, you tapped the table twice in this really cool and slow way, and the dealer burned another card and then dropped the Five of Diamonds on the turn.

"But this time," Lexie said with a grin, "there *were* bets. Rey pushed two hundred into the pot. Mark called it. And then it was back to you." She laughed nostalgically. "Oh my god, you could *feel* the tension in the room. But not from you. You looked so calm and composed—but deadly."

Dylan laughed. "Deadly?"

"Very," Lexie chuckled. "And handsome. Like that guy in that old poker movie, you know that one?"

"I know em all," Dylan said, unable to take his eyes off of hers.

"I'm being serious."

"I know you are."

She punched his shoulder, but he could tell that she wasn't really angry. "Do you want me to finish this story or not?"

"Yes," he said with serious eyes, but the smile still lingered at one corner of his mouth.

"It's a good one," she said. "You end up being the hero."

"I thought I was deadly."

"You *were* deadly . . . but only to villain."

"Mark!" Dylan said with feigned shock as if suddenly realizing who was the bad guy in Lexie's story.

Lexie paused. Then, with a coy smile, she said, "Maybe."

She was so beautiful, Dylan wanted to reach out and trace the outline of her face with his fingertips. But he kept his hands at his sides.

"So," Lexie said, "there you were, all deadly and handsome and heroic, holding everyone on the edge of their seats. And it was worth the wait because when you reached for your stack, it wasn't just for calling chips. You put together a 'put up or shut up' raise and slid it into the pot, nice and smoothly.

"Then everybody just sat there frozen, even the guys who'd already folded. They just sat there with their mouths hanging open. Except for Rey. He was really still and quiet. He was like you, taking the time to think about it. And after he thought about it, he called . . . which is exactly what you wanted him to do. I could see it in your eyes. The others couldn't—not even Rey, who, outside of you, was the most disciplined player at the table. But I could see it. And when everyone's eyes shifted to Mark, I already knew what he was going to do. I knew it just like you knew it."

"And what did he do?" Dylan asked, already knowing the answer but enjoying the story too much not to play along.

"He folded," Lexie said, no sign of guile in her expression. "He folded the best hand because you made him doubt himself. And when the Nine of Diamonds hit the river, he breathed a sigh of relief because he was sure you'd made your flush." She paused briefly. "And when you checked the river and left it to Rey to seal his own fate, Mark was almost gleeful that he'd thrown away his pocket Queens and couldn't wait to see you lower the boom on poor Rey. He really was a villain—Mark, not Rey."

Something flickered in Dylan's eyes—a scarcely discernible flicker, but Lexie saw it, and she nodded.

"But when Rey put out his modest value bet and you folded without really thinking, Mark was stunned. And when he asked Rey what he had and Rey turned over his pocket Jacks, Mark hit the roof. He flipped over his pocket Queens and started bitching about how he'd folded the winning hand to a measly pair of Jacks. Then he demanded that you show him your cards, and you just looked at him with that deadly gaze and said with a half smile, 'You should have called if you wanted to see them.' And Mark started bitching that the only reason he'd folded was because he thought you had the Ace. Or the Five. Or at least that you'd caught a diamond flush draw on the turn. He called you every name in the book and said you had no right to go running up the pot if you didn't have a hand worth calling a measly value bet. He really liked that word, 'measly'—especially when he was pissed, and, boy, was he pissed at you!"

It was true. Mark Jablonski had gone ballistic at the table and demanded Dylan show him his cards. But Lexie had brushed over the harsher edges of Mark's tirade. He had also accused Dylan of being in "collusion with the spic from the ghetto" and said it was no wonder, considering Dylan's family's history.

"His grandfather went to prison for colluding with the Russians and selling out America," Mark had seethed to the other players at the table. "And his great-grandfather ended up in the nut house. The whole family is a bunch of fuckin liars, cheaters, and crooks. His old man cheated his way into the fucking governor's mansion, and he'll probably cheat his way into the White House . . . just like Great-granddaddy did, ain't that right, Latner?"

Dylan had remained calm and composed throughout Mark's tantrum because most of what Mark had said was true (though, in his invective-laced diatribe, Mark neglected to mention that his own father was one of Dylan's dad's major campaign contributors). It was only when the ire of the loser was unleashed on the winner—Rey Peralta, whose sole offense had been playing the hand he was dealt—that Dylan stood up and went toe-to-toe with Mark.

Things hadn't gotten physical. Though Mark was built

like Dylan and ranked third statewide in wrestling, he knew better than to take the challenge any further. And when Dylan asked evenly if he was finished, Mark fixed him with a hard glare and then turned and stalked off without another word.

Dylan didn't counter Lexie's softened version of events. He just offered a humble smile. But Lexie wasn't buying it.

"I think you made your flush on the river," she said with a sparkle in her narrowed eyes. "And I think you folded to Rey's value bet, knowing that he only had a pair. I'm not sure if you knew that Mark had a better pair than Rey's pocket Jacks, but I *do* know that your raise on the turn was to ensure that Mark would fold whatever he was holding . . . and that by then, you'd already made your decision to fold to Rey, no matter what card hit the river."

Dylan grinned and shook his head. "Now why would I do something like that?"

Lexie said simply, "Because Rey was the underdog. And you're the good guy, and the good guy always stands up for the underdog."

Dylan shook his head again and said, "I'm not so good."

"You think you're the bad boy?"

"I didn't say that."

"But you think it."

Dylan looked at her, but he didn't respond.

"You think being the black sheep of the family—the outcast—automatically makes someone bad."

"Depends on what family you come from."

Lexie nodded. "Good answer."

Dylan shrugged. "Either way, it doesn't matter. Even if you're the black sheep of a bad family, that doesn't necessarily make you good."

She grinned with approval. "Touché."

Feeling slightly embarrassed, Dylan added, "I'm just saying."

Lexie studied him for a moment. With his tousled blond

hair and deep blue eyes, both troubled and steadfast at once, he looked more like his mother than his father. Lexie had only seen one photograph of Dylan's biological mother— a candid shot of her with Dylan at the age of four, taken shortly before her death. The photo had been taken by the gazebo on a sunny autumn day. Both mother and child were smiling. But while Dylan's smile lit up his adorable face, his mother's smile, though filled with obvious love for her child, did not reflect the joy of the moment. She had been a beautiful lingerie model when Dylan's father met her, and she was still beautiful enough to model at thirty-one—so beautiful, in fact, that close examination of this final photo of mother and son offered no clue that she was in stage four of breast cancer and had less than two months to live.

The quality of sadness in her eyes, which her smile had come close to concealing, had been inherited by Dylan. Since the day Lexie had first caught sight of him back in high school, no matter how light the occasion or circumstance, that same quality of sadness had always been there, lingering beneath the surface of his beautiful eyes.

Lexie pushed the image of the old photograph Charlie had shown her out of her mind, resolved to erase the sadness from Dylan's eyes, and with a suddenness that surprised Dylan, she said, "I want to see the bad boy."

Dylan squinted in confusion.

"Right now," she said. "I want to see this bad boy you think you are."

"I never said I was—"

"No, but you *think* it—and don't even try denying it. I want to see it, and you promised Charlie that you'd show me around."

"I did show you around," Dylan said with a bemused half-smile.

"No, you didn't," Lexie said, flatly. "You left out one room down here, and the entire upstairs." On Dylan's narrow-eyed expression, she added, "And we'll start with that one room down here. It's the one place I know that will definitely bring out the bad boy in you."

Dylan still wasn't sure if she was serious or joking. It was difficult to tell, but it was also one of the reasons he found himself drawn to her. The combination of spontaneity and mystery that she exuded was as intoxicating as it was confounding. And despite his natural inclination toward prudence, especially when interacting with an unfamiliar acquaintance, he couldn't resist the urge to follow this beautiful girl's lead.

While Lexie slipped out from under Hakhan's chin and gently lowered his head to the sofa cushion without waking him, Dylan turned to the bartender and said, "Would you keep an eye on him for me, James?"

"Sure thing, Dylan."

Dylan put a tip in the glass on the bar and took one last look at the cat and dog on the sofa. Hakhan stirred but didn't open his eyes. He sighed in his sleep and stretched out . . . just enough that his front paw was touching the tip of Akasha's tail. Dylan suspected she was still awake, but this time, no growl came from her throat, and her tail didn't twitch.

8

The crystal chandeliers of the Grand Atrium glistened dimly as Dylan crossed the threshold of the north entrance and looked around for Lexie. He spotted her near the south end of the room; she was making her way between the rows of gaming tables at a leisurely gait. Under other circumstances, Dylan would have immediately gravitated to such a beautiful girl at a party. But this was Lexie's game, and the rules had been clear. They were to enter the Atrium separately as "strangers" and mill about until they found the perfect "mark" before moving in for the "kill."

"The kill?" Dylan had asked with a raised brow.

"Yes, the kill," Lexie replied. "I thought you said you'd seen all the poker movies."

"I have, but we're not going to play poker."

Lexie made a face. "Same difference."

Dylan laughed.

"I'm serious," she said, punching him in the shoulder. She could tell by his smile that it didn't hurt, but she appreciated that he rubbed it as if it did. "I'm not a complete novice. I know what I'm talking about. I played Molly in our senior year production of *Molly's Game* at Overland."

"So, you're an actress?" Dylan said, his smile turning sly.

Lexie smiled sheepishly. "For about five minutes—but I was *good*. Ask Charlie. He came to all four performances."

"They closed you down after only four performances?"

She punched his shoulder again. This time it did hurt a little, but he couldn't stop smiling.

"It was a high school play—all they *do* is four performances!" She shook her head. "Anyway, the play is based on a true story, and the *real* Molly ran a back-room gambling ring that made *millions*. I know how to move in on a mark."

Dylan had not only been amused by Lexie's bravado but tantalized by the sparkle in her eyes, and so he hadn't bothered to explain to her that there was no "mark" at a legitimate casino; when it came to most table games, it was only you and three crucial factors: common sense, temperance, and a dash of Lady Luck.

The music spilling from the Atrium's speakers wasn't as loud as the thrumming party mix on the patio outside the Red Lounge, but the scintillating beat teased Dylan's senses and accelerated the flow of blood through his veins. It was one of Charlie's oldies, an Ed Sheeran tune, entitled *Don't*, which underscored Lexie's game perfectly, as if it had been deliberately selected for this moment.

Dylan followed Lexie's lead, meandering through the aisles between the gaming tables, casually surveying the action. Along the way, he couldn't help stealing occasional glances at Lexie. A couple of times, she caught him doing it but remained cool and focused on the task of finding their "mark." Once, they even came close enough to brush shoulders, and though the thrill of being so near her sent waves of tendrils racing over his skin, Dylan kept his composure, and per the rules, neither he nor Lexie offered one another so much as a glance. They remained strangers who had yet to connect over the right table.

Up in the dimly lit control room on the mezzanine level of the residence, Charlie sat before a bank of monitors, his eyes flitting from screen to screen, scanning the activity in the Atrium below.

His sight locked on a single monitor which offered a crisp shot of Dylan approaching a craps table at the center of the hall. Then his eyes flitted to another monitor which displayed the opposite end of the table where Lexie stood with her hands resting on the cushioned rail. Charlie flipped a switch on the control panel, and the separate images of his brother and Lexie appeared on the two center screens, side by side. He pressed a button on his headset and said softly, "Do you have the sparrow?"

On another monitor, the croupier across the table from the boxman scooped up the dice with his stick and nodded his head as if to the beat of the music. After a cursory examination of the dice, he called out to the boxman, "Capped die."

The boxman nodded without looking up from the chips he was stacking, and the croupier discarded the used dice and broke the seal on a fresh pack.

In the control room, Charlie spoke into his headset again. "Go."

Down on the floor, the player to Lexie's immediate right collected his chips and left the table, while in the darkened room above, Charlie turned up the music a notch.

Dylan stood now at the opposite end of the crowded craps table, his gaze on Lexie. He didn't expect her to acknowledge him—she was far too committed to her role-playing game for that. But he was looking for a sign, which came in short order. With a meticulously manicured fingernail, Lexie surreptitiously tapped the cushioned rail once, and as he reached into his pocket for his money clip, Dylan couldn't help smiling at how much she was enjoying their little "deception."

The croupier set the fresh dice on the felt and used his stick to move them down the table toward Lexie while announcing, "New shooter. Comin' out lucky for the lovely lady in red. The field is green, don't be shy."

While Lexie examined the dice, Dylan laid a couple of twenties on the felt, and the dealer to the left of the boxman gave him a stack of chips. Lexie chose her dice, and the stick came across the table to scoop up the remaining three.

Lexie's come-out roll was a seven, and the crowd around the table cheered as they collected their winnings. They went wild when her next three rolls all came up seven.

The point was established on Lexie's fifth roll, with a nine. The crowd cheered again but not as vigorously as before; they were hoping for a six or an eight.

Dylan smiled because nine was his favorite point number; though its odds of hitting were 1.8 percent less than a six or an eight hitting, its payout was four times greater on a bet placed behind the original pass-line bet. He'd had $10 on the pass-line for Lexie's four come out rolls, and now as the croupier to the right of the boxman turned the dealer button over and moved it to the box marked "NINE" on the felt, Dylan placed another $20 behind his original bet. Now all Lexie had to do was avoid rolling another seven, which, after the point has been established, is craps and would end her run.

As it turned out, her run was a long one, and though Dylan wasn't betting large like he had the other night at the old man's casino, he pulled down a tidy profit.

But it wasn't profit that concerned him. It was the joy

in Lexie's smile, the intoxicating sound of her laughter, the sparkle in her eyes. Of all the girls he'd ever dated, he honestly couldn't recall a single one who'd made him feel so alive, so curious to plumb the depths of her mystery and discover her deepest secrets.

And while he certainly enjoyed his vantage point, which offered a breathtaking view of Lexie's performance, he suddenly realized that what he really wanted was to be standing next to her at the opposite end of the table. He wanted to feel the heat coming off of her as she threw the dice. He wanted her to throw her arms around him each time she rolled another nine. He wanted to feel her breath close to his ear, whispering something silly like "They're onto us, we'll have to make a run for it."

Dylan blushed at the absurd image that suddenly popped up in his mind—the two of them racing from the casino like Bonnie and Clyde with the loot—and his color only deepened when he noticed Lexie smiling at him from the far end of the table as if she could read his thoughts.

By the time Lexie's roll came to an end, their combined winnings totaled a little over six hundred, the greater sum of which sat at Dylan's end of the table. Lexie, who had never played craps before, hadn't placed any free-odds bets as Dylan had; she'd just put $10 on the pass-line and collected her winnings as they came in. It was a good system because it allowed the shooter to remain loose and carefree while her "partner in crime" quietly raked in the "big bucks" at the opposite end of the table.

But the amount she'd won hadn't mattered to Lexie; the real thrill had come from throwing the dice and hitting the point number 11 out of 31 rolls.

They left the table separately and met up on their way to the cashier's cage. Only then did Lexie drop her cover and release a low, conspiratorial laugh.

"Did you see that? They had no clue we were in on it

together!" Her eyes suddenly grew large. "We have to do this again! We'll hit every casino between here and Atlantic City. Then, after we've fleeced them all, we'll head out for the big one: Vegas! No. Monte Carlo!" She shook her head quickly. "No. First Vegas. *Then* Monte Carlo. We'll need to hone our skills to perfection—Monte Carlo is loaded with crafty dealers! We can't take any chances. How's your French?"

Dylan winced with a guilty smile. Lexie rolled her eyes in disbelief and laughed.

"That's OK. I know enough for the both of us. I can give you a crash course on the road." Her energy was soaring sky-high, and as they waited in line, she fired off the details of her plan to make millions ("scratch that—billions") off of the casinos. Dylan only interrupted once, to remind her that not every table paid off like the one they'd just hit.

"It's the law of diminishing returns," he cautioned.

"That's just the point," she said, her eyes flaring brilliantly. "We're not going to *obey* the laws! We're outlaws! They don't stand a chance against us!"

Dylan couldn't argue with her logic. Or maybe it was just her vibrant smile and those stunning green eyes that seemed to look straight into his soul without flinching or trying to unpack all the buried baggage.

At the cage, Dylan set his tall stack of chips next to Lexie's shorter stack and requested a check for the entire amount made out in Lexie's name.

"No way," Lexie countered at once. "This was a team effort—and anyway, you risked more than I did."

"I think I can afford the forty bucks," Dylan said with an easy smile.

"Uh-uh," Lexie said, and she turned to the cashier. "We'll take it in cash. Split fifty-fifty."

"I don't really need the money."

Lexie's comeback was swift and smooth: "And what makes you think I do?"

Dylan's cheeks flushed. "I didn't mean it that way—"

"Relax, Galahad," Lexie said as she took her winnings and handed Dylan his. "I'm not a snowflake. I'm an iceberg. And we're a team now. No more passing me in the halls at school without a second glance—not that I'm holding any grudges, mind you. Things are different now. And there's no going back." She stopped and raised a brow. "Unless you want to? No hard feelings, I can take a hint. You don't have to hit me over the head with a mallet."

Dylan was looking deeply into her eyes now. He didn't want to go back. He wanted to go forward, wherever she planned to lead him.

"Alrighty then," she said with a nod. "I believe you still owe me a tour of the upstairs . . . unless you're a welsher, in which case I'm gonna have to rethink that fifty-fifty split."

Up in the control room, Charlie watched as Dylan and Lexie made their way toward the Atrium's south exit. When they disappeared from view, Charlie turned away from the monitor, retrieved his suit jacket from the coat tree, and headed out into the quiet hallway.

It was 9:27 P.M. and things were moving along at a steady tick. There was more than enough time before the curtain rose on the midnight show.

9

The tour of the upstairs residence went by swiftly—the only room they lingered in was "The Armory," so dubbed by Dylan and Charlie's older brothers, who were both avid hunters and collectors of all manner of weaponry. Dylan had never cared for this room, but Lexie found it intriguing and perused its walls with a decided eye for the more exotic weapons—swords, daggers, bolos, spears, staffs, axes, maces, and countless others she'd never seen before. With a glance at Dylan, she said, "I take it you're not into all this."

Dylan shook his head with a half smile. But when his sight lit on the set of crossbows on display above the mantle, something shifted inside him, and his gaze went a shade dark. Most people wouldn't have noticed this shift; but then Lexie wasn't most people.

"He told me about the deer," she said. "Charlie," she added, though it was clear Dylan understood just who the "he" she'd referred to was. She waited a moment, and then said, "At first, he tried to act like it hadn't affected him, but

I could tell that it had." She shook her head with an ironic half-chuckle. "I guess stoicism runs in the family."

Dylan nodded, his gaze still on the crossbows above the mantle. He hadn't known about the hunting trip until a few weeks after when he'd come home from college for the weekend. Charlie was holed up in his room, Morgana was silently seething, and the old man and his two older sons were suspiciously silent at the dinner table. When Dylan had finally had enough and asked what was going on, Morgana obligingly spilled the beans.

"The stupids," she said in her thick accent. "They take him to kill the baby deer, and he watch it suffer because the bow slip and the arrow doesn't kill, just wound, and he is too young to be killing the babies. No one should be killing the babies deer. There, I say it, so sue me."

It ended up being another memorable family dinner where the only one left at the table was Morgana.

As usual, the old man was the first one out. When Dylan started in on his older brothers, the old man attempted to intercede. But things turned ugly fast.

Dylan told their father to stay out of it.

Brady snorted indignantly. "You can't tell Dad what to do."

Tom echoed the sentiment. "You have no right to disrespect our father."

The old man slammed his silverware onto his plate. "Then I'll *leave* my own fucking house." And pointing a finger at his older sons, he added, "And don't anybody even *think* about following me. I need fuckin' *peace* when I'm eating. I don't need this crazy shit, and I'm *not* getting indigestion for any of you!"

Brady and Tom sat at the table as the old man stormed out. Though considerably older than Dylan, both were tall and lanky like Charlie, and neither came close to matching Dylan in strength. Things didn't get physical, but words were exchanged, and in the end, the two older brothers were cowed by the younger and sat silently fuming as Dylan told them in no uncertain terms what would happen if they ever tried to rope Charlie into another hunting trip.

"Are we clear, Brady?"

"Yes," Brady said, looking down at his plate.

"Yes, what?"

"Yes, Dylan," Brady said through clenched teeth. "We are clear. We will never take him hunting again. Satisfied?"

He'd left them both at the table with Morgana, but on his way down the hall to Charlie's room, he could hear Tom saying, "If that fucker ever lays a hand on me, I'll sue. Fuck family, I swear to god, I'll sue."

Still looking up at the crossbows, Dylan recalled Charlie leaning into his shoulder as they sat side by side on Charlie's bed. The shield of stoicism that the kid put up for everyone else was gone, and hot tears were spilling down his cheeks as he buried his face in Dylan's shoulder and said, "I killed her, Dylan, I killed the little deer . . . I tried to stop at the last second—I didn't want to do it—but I pulled the trigger, and I killed her, and she cried, she was crying out, it was so awful, she kept crying and crying, and I couldn't save her because I did that . . . *I* did that to her . . . "

"He didn't do it," Lexie said, snapping Dylan out of the memory. "One of the other hunters killed the deer. He just wounded it. He's not like them. He's gentle and kind. You know that, right?"

Dylan looked up at the crossbows one last time and nodded. Then he followed Lexie out of the room.

Down the hall, they came upon the opulent master suite, which was currently unoccupied. Normally, Morgana and the old man would be here on New Year's Eve, but after the election, Morgana had made arrangements for them to spend the holidays at *Marina di Portofino*. The family had gathered on Christmas Eve at the Tower K penthouse in New York. Then after an early dinner and gift exchange, Morgana and the old man had taken the private jet to

Portofino Bay so that they could wake up on Christmas morning to see the sunrise on the Italian Riviera. Back when the boys were younger, they would sometimes accompany their father and stepmother on vacations. But Dylan was out of the nest now, and Charlie was almost seventeen, so he was left to throw his New Year's bash down here in Palm Beach without supervision.

"Do they do that often," Lexie inquired.

"What? Leave their minor children unsupervised in the adult playground?" He offered a smile that didn't quite reach his eyes and said, "Yeah, that's pretty standard. But you get used to it growing up around here."

They were headed toward the Solarium, which was really the only sight worth seeing in the upper levels of the residence—at least in Dylan's opinion, it was—when Lexie halted and said, "Hey, you didn't show me *your* room!"

Dylan looked nonplussed. "It's pretty much like all the other rooms you saw."

"Yeah, but I still want to see it. I want to see where you grew up."

Dylan smiled curiously. "I grew up in New York, just like you."

"But not in the summertime. I want to see where you spent your summer vacations."

Dylan grinned. "It's not like I was holed up in my room the entire time. I got out occasionally."

Lexie smiled that beautiful smile of hers and rolled her eyes. "I know that, silly. But I still want to see it. I want to see where you practiced that irresistible brooding charm of yours." She made a serious face with brooding eyes, and Dylan laughed.

"I don't look like that."

"Yes, you do. You look exactly like this." She made the face again, and Dylan nodded.

"All right, you got me there," he agreed, his cheeks flushing. "I concede."

But Lexie was having too much fun. She made a sad, brooding, serious face, and Dylan laughed again.

"All right," he said, "stop making that face, and I'll show you my room."

Lexie giggled. "I like it when you make that face. It's sexy. Makes you look like a model." Dylan rolled his eyes, and she said, "*I'd* buy a magazine with you on the cover." She turned her head slightly and gave him another brooding model look.

"OK, that's it," he said, turning away, but when she took his arm and pulled him back to face her, he was smiling. "Are you finished?"

"Maybe," she said with a mischievous grin.

Dylan rolled his eyes and turned away again, but in truth, he was enjoying it. In fact, in his entire life, he'd never met a girl who had so instantly captivated and intrigued him at once.

His bedroom was a little smaller than the others he'd shown her, and far more modestly decorated. Lexie suspected he'd chosen it for its distance from the master suite and its proximity to the service stairwell. She imagined him as a boy, stealthily sneaking down those stairs on late summer nights while the rest of the family was asleep and escaping by way of the kitchen door; perhaps stopping at the fridge to get a snack to enjoy under the stars.

The room contained only the necessities, and all was tidy and organized as if a maid came in regularly to vacuum and dust (which indeed was the case; Morgana was a neatness freak and insisted that every last corner of the residence be kept spotless).

The bookcase next to Dylan's desk was filled with academic volumes, a few of which Lexie remembered from school, and an assortment of other books, some of which she'd read, others that she'd only heard of—*The Basketball Diaries, The Sellout, In Search of Lost Time, The Quiet American, The Library of Babel & Other Stories, The Last Picture Show,*

East of Eden, The Lowland, A Place Called Freedom—along with numerous collections of poetry by authors like Terrance Hayes, Gabriela Mistral, Billy Collins, Jimmy Santiago Baca, Keorapetse Kgositsile.

At the bottom of the shelf, there were four oversized volumes that she recognized at once. They were Dylan's high school yearbooks; the one from his senior year was identical to the one on her own bookshelf back home in New York, but the three other volumes were from a time before she had entered her freshman year.

Lexie turned her attention from the bookcase to the poster on the wall above the desk. The black and white image of an old man with kind eyes and a warm smile looked back at her. The quote below the image read:

> *"I never lose. I either win or learn."*
> —Madiba

Lexie tipped a scarcely discernible nod to the old man on the poster, her eyes twinkling with approval. Then with a glance back at the Kgositsile poetry books, she quoted, *"'In a situation of oppression, there are no choices beyond didactic writing: either you are a tool of oppression or an instrument of liberation.'"*

"Impressive," Dylan said with a grin of approval.

"I'm down with Bra Willie," Lexie came back smoothly. She took another casual look around the sparsely decorated room. "So, you prefer to live with the bare minimum . . . "

Dylan didn't respond; it was an observation, not a question. His eyes remained focused on her. She turned her head and pierced him gently with her gaze. His stomach did a somersault, but he stood steady.

"You're not a monk, are you?" she asked with an unreadable smile. "You haven't like forsaken all worldly possessions for a higher calling or something . . . "

Dylan shook his head and pushed a smile as his heart

pounded a slow, driving drumbeat in his chest. Everything was still for a moment as the two of them stood in the quiet bedroom looking at one another.

Then Lexie walked toward him, and his heartbeat accelerated. But she didn't stop in front of him as he'd expected. She walked right past him to the open door. He waited to hear her footsteps in the hallway, moving toward their next stop on the tour. But she didn't leave the room. And the next sound wasn't her footfalls in the hallway; it was the door closing.

And then the lights dimmed, and the room was illuminated by the misty glow of the full moon spilling through the French doors that led out to the balcony. And shortly, soft music came from somewhere in the darkness.

Dylan stood with his back to the door, uncertain—not of himself; he knew what he wanted. But he wasn't sure about Lexie. With a girl like her, he could imagine turning around to find her laughing and saying something like, "Oh my god, you should see the look on your face!" Not in a mean-spirited way—she wasn't a mean-spirited girl. Just a little good-natured teasing to get him to loosen up and not take everything so seriously.

Dylan wasn't sure if he was ready for something like that, but he resolved to smile and even laugh right along with her because it was true. He was pretty tightly wound and perhaps needed to loosen up and have a healthy laugh at himself.

But when he turned around, Lexie wasn't standing at the door pointing at him and laughing that delightful laugh of hers. She was standing right there behind him. And now they were face to face.

The sudden closeness caused Dylan's heart to skip a beat, and his lips parted. But before he could utter a sound, Lexie placed a gentle forefinger to his lips and whispered, "I want to see those tattoos."

. . .

In the shadows of the closet, Charlie stood perfectly still, breathing short, soundless breaths as he watched the scene unfolding in his older brother's bedroom. He was surprised by the precise mechanics of the seduction. It wasn't that he'd expected Dylan to be a clumsy brute, exerting his alpha male dominance over Lexie with his strong, hard body. But he *had* expected that Dylan would take on the more assertive role of the experienced paramour, leading with his mouth as well as his hands, skillfully coaxing the girl into his bed.

But it wasn't like that at all. It was Lexie who took charge and set the rhythm of the tryst.

They stood in the center of the room, Dylan facing the shaft of moonlight that spilled through the sheers over the French doors, Lexie lit by the glow of the stereo system. She had plugged her phone into the stereo and set a mix track going. A dreamy cover of Springsteen's *I'm on Fire* by AWOLNATION filled the room as the two of them stood with their foreheads touching and swayed to the gentle rhythm . . . while from his hiding place in the closet, Charlie peered through the slats of the louvered door and thought, *They're almost dancing.*

His heart skipped a beat when Lexie reached up and touched Dylan's face, and when her fingertips moved back into Dylan's hair and she rose up on her toes to reach Dylan's lips, Charlie felt a thrill race through his body. The kiss lingered—tentative at first, then probing—and Charlie licked his dry lips.

Without breaking from the kiss, Lexie maneuvered Dylan to the bed. When she placed her hands on Dylan's shoulders, he went with the motion and sat on the edge of the bed. They stayed like this for a moment, Lexie standing between Dylan's legs as he gazed up into her eyes with a mixture of desire and obedience. Then Lexie took hold of the hem of Dylan's shirt, and he raised his arms above his head while she pulled it off him.

As the shirt fell to the floor, Charlie felt a sharp sensation near his heart, as if an invisible blade had slid between his ribs. Dylan had always had an enviable physique, even before he'd started lifting weights with his buddies in high school. Charlie supposed it was a genetic trait Dylan had been blessed with from his mother's side of the family—it certainly hadn't come from their father, who like Charlie, had been tall and lanky most of his life (Father's gut hadn't come until his early forties when his indulgence of sweets and fast food finally caught up with him).

Charlie could not remember a time when Dylan wasn't perfect, and looking at Dylan's exposed upper body, with all the curves and lines in all the right places, he was reminded once again of his own physical shortcomings. Though he had never resented his older brother's seemingly effortless attributes, he had envied them more than he would ever care to admit to another living soul.

Charlie remembered the one time he had come close to divulging his secret envy to Dylan. It had happened while they were on holiday in Catalina (Father had wanted to leave them at home with Lupita, but Morgana had insisted on a family Christmas). Dylan had just turned seventeen and Charlie was two months shy of his thirteenth birthday. They had just come ashore from a refreshing swim and were basking under the warm midday sunshine when Charlie noticed a group of girls down the beach watching them. They were around Charlie's age, and every time he looked in their direction, they turned away with bashful smiles and giggled.

Charlie knew who they were looking at, and it wasn't him. Girls had never shown the slightest bit of interest in Charlie—certainly not while Dylan was around. Charlie looked out at the shimmering blue water and with a suddenness that surprised him asked Dylan, "What does it feel like to be beautiful?"

Dylan made a face like it was the most baffling question he'd ever heard. "What's that supposed to mean?"

"You know . . ." He tipped a surreptitious nod in the direction of the girls down the beach. " . . . having girls look at you like that all the time. What does it feel like?"

Dylan laughed—not cruelly, more like he'd just heard a confounding joke. When Charlie asked what was so funny, Dylan said, "They're not looking at me, you dope. They're looking at you. Especially the cute little redhead—she likes that whole dark and brooding Henry Jennings from *The Americans* vibe you put out."

Now it was Charlie's turn to look confused.

"Forget it," Dylan said, "it's before your time." Then without so much as a side glance at the girls, he added, "See the way they keep looking away and giggling whenever you look at them? They think you're cute. Trust me."

Charlie looked even more confused. No one had ever told him he was cute, and hearing it for the first time from his older brother, who'd been voted by his senior class Best Eyes, Best Hair, Best Smile, Best Body, Best Looking, and Best Personality, was a bit jarring.

Dylan smiled and said, "You could ask her to the Tree Lighting Ceremony tonight. I'll bet you she'd accept."

Charlie smiled, despite himself. But he didn't respond.

"I could go over there and ask her for you if you want," Dylan said with a tempting grin. "I could say, 'Hey, you see that cute guy over there with the dark hair and brooding eyes who looks like Henry from *The Americans*? He's my brother, and he thinks you're really pretty, and he'd like to ask you to the ceremony tonight.'"

Charlie hadn't asked the pretty redheaded girl to the ceremony that night, and he hadn't let Dylan do it either.

As he stood in the shadows of the closet now, watching

his older brother and another pretty redheaded girl doing things that he himself had never done—except in his fantasies—he thought of that moment on the beach four years ago and wondered if his life would be different if he had worked up the courage to approach the girl who'd stolen glances at him and smiled that sweet, bashful smile.

He wondered if he would be hiding in the closet and spying on this intimate moment between his brother and Lexie right now if he had just manned-up on that beach and asked the pretty girl to join him at the ceremony. Had he missed out on a crucial developmental moment? Could something that simple have changed the course of his life? Could it have made him normal like Dylan?

A voice suddenly chimed in, *Normal isn't normal, dear.*

For a second, Charlie froze, fearful that he had spoken those words aloud. But it wasn't his voice. It was his grandmother's voice. And it was only inside his head.

Grandmother Lona (or as she was affectionately referred to by family and friends alike: Grandmama—properly pronounced "Grand-muh-MAH") was his father's mother. At seventy-five, she was hearty and hale and still stood tall, with her back straight and her chin held high. But more important, she controlled the family's vast wealth (which had been significantly increased by her father's turbulent tenure in the Oval Office, which had been long before Charlie and Dylan were born), and so, when she spoke—even if it was only inside your head—you stopped and paid attention because no one in the family possessed more power and wisdom than Grandmama Lona.

Charlie adored his grandmother and was fond of her many personal colloquialisms, such as "Normal isn't normal" and "Facts can be deceiving." He even liked the ones whose full meanings eluded his grasp: "Truth is relative to perspective," "Logic only serves to cloud the clear mind and prevent decisive action," and "What we see through the lens of impartiality is often skewed by those whose agenda diverges from our own." Grandmama Lona frequently dispatched wisdom in the esoteric, and as a dutiful grandson, Charlie had never dared to challenge her acumen.

This was not to say that his grandmother was an irascible woman. Indeed she was, without exception, the most pleasant of women, even when roundly vexed.

But, as Charlie had learned from a very young age, Grandmama Lona was not one to be questioned. When she offered advice or delivered a proclamation, you simply accepted it. Those foolish enough to challenge her authority were met with nothing more than a cool gaze and a thin smile. And only later—weeks, months, sometimes even years—would they receive Grandmama Lona's delayed response to their infraction. For family members, this would usually come in the form of a birthday check in the amount of five cents, as in a nickel's worth of advice. As always, the check would be tucked into a lovely card, but in addition to her signature—*Love always, Grandmama*—there would be a message like *So appreciative of your input!* or *In loving gratitude of your advice!* For less fortunate souls—those outside the family circle—there would be a pink slip (also tucked into a lovely card), with a message like *Heartfelt appreciation for your years of faithful service* or *Ever in debt to your priceless advice and loyal assistance.* These cards with their pink bombs inside would invariably make their way through the post to arrive just before the holidays.

By far, Charlie's favorite of Grandmama Lona's sayings was "One man's complicity is another man's justice."

Though he didn't fully understand this one any more than her countless other maxims, he believed it nonetheless and reasoned that, at its core, it meant: a questionable action was not necessarily a crime just because others—even the majority of others—saw it that way. And with this in mind, he believed his Grandmama Lona would approve of what he was doing right now . . . or at least that she wouldn't be disappointed enough to send him a five cent birthday check this coming March.

Charlie snapped out of his reverie when the Springsteen cover faded and the next track on Lexie's mobile phone came on—a poppy Ed Sheeran tune called *Shape of You*.

Charlie watched in a near trancelike state as Lexie's hands and mouth moved over his older brother's body. Teasing, testing, smiling deliciously at Dylan's every wince as she discovered his ticklish spots with her tongue. She held both of his wrists down to the bed, even though there was no need to restrain him. Dylan was far too much of a gentleman to interrupt or prevent her from taking what she desired. But as predictable as Dylan's response to Lexie's advance was, Charlie found his brother's complete and total supplication not only surprising but also a bit disconcerting, and he couldn't help feeling impatient for Dylan to take over or at least reciprocate.

The tantalizing yet maddeningly frustrating foreplay went on for the duration of the Ed Sheeran song—a slow strip tease, which left Dylan and Lexie in nothing but their underwear. But things took a turn when the next song—The Weeknd's *Earned It*—came on.

The look in Dylan's eyes suddenly shifted from dreamy supplication to active desire, and as he unfastened Lexie's bra, her hand slid into his boxers, and their lips met hungrily.

In the shadows of the closet, Charlie's heart began to slam against the wall of his skinny chest, and he reached for the swell that pressed urgently at his trousers. He didn't unzip his fly or reach inside his underwear—if he'd done that, it would have been over in an instant. Instead, he worked the swell through his trousers with the palm of his open hand in long, slow strokes while taking short, silent breaths. He didn't want to reach climax before it was over.

On the bed now, Dylan and Lexie were completely

naked, kissing, caressing, grinding, but not yet in coitus. Lexie's hands kept moving over Dylan's body, guiding him, controlling him, making him seem *diminished*, and Dylan kept allowing it, following her lead. Even when he took her breasts into his powerful hands and kissed them, tasted them, he didn't appear in control—at least not in the way Charlie wanted him to be. He wanted Dylan to get on top of her—or better, to force her face-down on the bed, hike her ass up, and take her from behind. But Dylan was not that kind of lover. He was strong and passionate, but, at the same time, gentle and attentive to Lexie's needs and desires.

In spite of the louvered slats on the closet door, the air was dense, and Charlie had begun to break a sweat. He felt it on his forehead and beneath his Eton twill shirt, running down the line of his back. He loosened his tie and unfastened the top button of his shirt while continuing to rub the stiff swell in his trousers in a slightly more aggressive manner. Part of him—a secret place inside his mind that sometimes frightened him—wanted to burst from the closet, pull the Salvatore Ferragamo belt from his waist, lash Dylan's wrists to the bedpost with it, and make him watch how to do it properly. He imagined Dylan trying to escape while he, Charlie, the younger and supposedly weaker brother, forced Lexie down onto the bed—or better, the floor—and put it to her good and hard. And when it was over, and his dominance was established, he would turn to Dylan and say, *Take it easy; it's not like you haven't seen it before . . . and you couldn't do anything about it then either, because* you're *the weak one.*

As that secret place within his mind reveled at the thought of putting Dylan in his place, the rest of Charlie shivered in revulsion. A hot tear spilled down his cheek as he continued to rub at the swell, faster now because Dylan was inside of Lexie, and the rhythm of his thrust was building to something monumental. And Lexie was moving with that rhythm, giving herself over to it as she clung to Dylan and released a moan of ecstasy.

Charlie wanted to moan with her—he wanted to place his lips close to her ear and moan the words *I love you, and I will never hurt you*—but he bit his tongue and just kept working it right along with them. And when the climax came, Charlie slid to the closet floor and bit his fist to keep from crying out.

He had no idea how long he'd sat there—for a time it felt as if time itself had no meaning. But eventually—after Dylan and Lexie had got dressed and the sound of their footfalls had faded down the hallway outside the closed bedroom door—Charlie released a shuddering sigh.

Shortly, he collected himself before heading off to the private bath in his own room for a quick shower and fresh change of clothes.

But this was only a slight detour.

The night was far from over, and the real climax was yet to come.

10

The Solarium was cloaked in shadow, its polished maple floor streaked with spidery veins of brilliant moonlight, as filtered through the stained glass dome at the center of the high ceiling. Dylan arrived at half past eleven. He had escorted Lexie back to the ground floor of the residence and left her in the Red Lounge, with the promise that he would return after his meeting with Charlie. Lexie had smiled and assured him that she would hold him to that promise because she fully expected a New Year's kiss at the stroke of midnight. Dylan surprised himself by responding with a teasing grin: "I already gave you a New Year's kiss."

Lexie laughed and scolded, "Don't make me come and find you!"

Dylan was still smiling as he climbed the spiral staircase that opened onto the darkened Solarium, but when he spotted Charlie at the southeast curve of the glass-walled circular room, his smile faltered.

Charlie stood with his back to Dylan, his gaze fixed on the dark vista of Largo Morta's sprawling grounds. The first thing Dylan noticed was that Charlie had changed clothes since their last encounter a few hours ago, and his hair was damp as if he'd recently showered. The second thing he noticed was the stillness of Charlie's tall and narrow frame, and this gave Dylan pause.

Then from the silence, Charlie spoke.

"I know that you're leaving," he said in an oddly flat tone. "But when were you going to tell me that you'd dropped out of school?"

Dylan hadn't told anyone about leaving school; he hadn't even officially dropped out yet. He'd just planned to take off for parts unknown out West and never look back. He held his gaze on Charlie but didn't respond. There wasn't much to say now that Charlie already knew the truth.

Charlie took a breath and said in that same flat tone, "Five months, and you would have had your degree in Constitutional Law." He raised a brow at the flicker of Dylan's eyes reflected in the darkened glass wall beside his own reflection. "You didn't think we'd be able to find out that you'd switched your major from business to law, Dylan?" He paused again. "Do you think we're farmers? Bumpkins? Grandmother foots the bills, and she keeps an eagle eye on all of her investments, both large and small, and tuition at Harvard is no small investment, as I'm sure you are well aware."

Dylan stood silent.

Charlie took another breath and then turned his head to one side. "We're not upset with you, Dylan. We're your family, and we love you. We will always love you. And we will always be your family—regardless of where you go, what you do, whether or not you return our love. You belong to us. You are one of us. And nothing can change that. Nothing. Not ever." He turned his head back to the window and raised his chin as he gazed out at the night once again. "You're a Latner. And by extension, a Kingley. And as such, you have a responsibility to behave in a manner that reflects well upon the family." Another breath, another lift of the chin. "You may do as you wish in private—God knows, Father does—but your public face is our public face, and it must be unblemished. It must be."

Charlie's lips curled bitterly, and his eyes shined darkly in the glass, while behind him, Dylan remained silent. The shock had evaporated, and now Dylan's eyes were filled with sadness for his younger brother. Still, he didn't know what to say. It had never been his intention to hurt Charlie. He just needed to get away. For his own wellbeing.

Charlie straightened his spine and collected his emotions before going on. "Grandmother is actually proud of you. She's happy that you turned from business management to law. She knows that the family business isn't for you. She sees greater things in your future. Mine as well." He smiled a razor-thin smile, which looked ghostly in the darkened glass. "Father doesn't know anything about your academic shift, of course. But Grandmother can handle him. She's been doing it since long before either of us was ever born. Grandmother *sees* things—she has a canny eye for that. And she knows how to make things happen. She has the power to make things happen, and if you'd only—"

"Charlie . . ." Dylan began, but Charlie cut him off before he could get any further.

"Five months, Dylan. Five months, and you'll have your degree. And if you still feel the same way by then, I won't say anything. I won't try to interfere. You have my word."

"It's not that simple," Dylan said gently.

"It *is* that simple. You can *make* it that simple. Things only become difficult when people make them difficult, and there's nothing difficult about this."

"It's more complicated than that," Dylan said in that same gentle tone. "I have to—"

"No, Dylan, it's not. It's very *un*complicated. It's very

clear. That's why you're having so much trouble seeing it. You've always been overly analytical—particularly when it comes to practical matters. Grandmother sees things far more clearly. She knows that Father was a mistake—his *candidacy* was a mistake. It's a rigged system. He didn't stand a chance against *her*. She has all the dirty Liberal money and connections. This was nothing more than revenge against our great-grandfather for beating her grandmother, don't you see that? And Father, despite all his undeniable attributes, is definitely *not* the man his grandfather was."

Charlie stopped and shook his head as he gazed into the darkness of the night beyond the glass wall. Dylan waited, hoping that his kid brother would wind down the spiral as he used to after exhausting himself when they were younger. But Charlie's energy spiked again, and an ugly bitterness surfaced this time.

"He was so close to greatness, Dylan," Charlie said in a tightly controlled tone that bordered a whisper. "He came so close to making this country great again. He gave it everything he had, even as they chipped away at him, piece by piece. Even as they put everyone around him in prison, including our grandfather, who had done so much to reform the system, end the opioid crisis, and bring peace to the Middle East—it was so crazy in the Middle East back then, and our grandfather did so much to bring about peace. And he *would* have succeeded if the Deep State hadn't got to him and locked him up on trumped up charges—since when is it illegal to help your father-in-law get elected president? How could something so noble be illegal? How was it *his* fault that the Russians had dirt on *her*, can you tell me that?"

Dylan's response came softly but with certainty. "There was a little more to it than that, Charlie."

But Charlie just shook his head, with his lips pressed tightly together. "If he'd just avoided that trap. One trap. That's all he needed to do. If only he could have seen that it was a setup. But he couldn't resist the media—they were his only weakness. He wanted so badly for them to love him—couldn't they see that? But they were dead set against him from the beginning. They hated him for his politics, but they never failed to welcome him for the ratings he brought them."

Dylan realized that Charlie was no longer talking about their grandfather, who had been notoriously shy of media attention and scrutiny. He was talking about their great-grandfather, Grandmama Lona's father, the 45th President of the United States of America, who had spent his final years not in prison for his many crimes but in an asylum for the clinically insane.

"He wasn't prepared," Charlie said. "Nothing could have prepared him for that night . . . "

Charlie was speaking now of the night their great-grandfather, as the sitting President of the United States, had agreed to negotiate with the masked terrorist who had abducted his son-in-law, Charlie and Dylan's grandfather, Jacob Latner, Sr. It had been a disastrous circus from start to finish, and when the dust had finally settled, their great-grandfather's presidency had collapsed like a house of cards. And in short order, the old man himself had gone down. The official diagnosis had been "mid-stage dementia," but everyone who had witnessed the shocking climax of the President's encounter with the masked terrorist on live TV knew the truth. The President's mind, which had already been teetering on the brink of instability, had finally snapped.

"How could it be that simple?" Charlie said softly now as he gazed at his reflection in the darkened glass wall. "How could someone just put on a mask and hold the world captive like that? Hold the most powerful man in the world completely captive on live TV while every living soul in every country in the world watched, breathlessly hanging on every single moment. How could it be that simple to destroy the life achievements of a great man in a single night?"

Charlie stopped abruptly and shook his head in disbelief while a bitter smile crept across his lips.

"Oh, he wasn't your average terrorist with a bomb or a box-cutter looking to fly a jet into the side of a skyscraper, I'll give him that much. He had a certain flair for the dramatic, and his playlist was impeccable—every song carefully selected to tease, lure, and incite—but to . . . to *humiliate* the leader of the free world on live TV like that. To pick away at him slowly, methodically—*wantonly*—and then crush him like a bug. No respect. No remorse. Tangling our great-grandfather's words, twisting the truth, making him look like a *fool* on international TV. Deceitful, duplicitous, conniving, vile, foul, filthy, treacherous traitor . . . "

Charlie was trembling now, his hands balled into white-knuckled fists at his sides. Dylan's heart went out to him, but he also feared that in such a state Charlie might lose it and hurt himself. It had only happened a few times before, but one of those times ended up with a trip to the emergency room and thirteen stitches across the knuckles of Charlie's left hand after he'd driven his fist into a bathroom mirror.

Dylan attempted to calm him. "That was a long time ago, Charlie. Long before we were born. It's got nothing to do with us—"

"It has *everything* to do with us," Charlie seethed. "It's part of our history. That darkness—that *deficiency*—is in our blood. It's part of our *legacy*. You can't afford to be that blind, Dylan. Either one of us could be afflicted. We've both harbored dark thoughts toward Father. You said yourself that you would have killed him that day when he . . . the thing with Mother, you know. You said if you'd had a gun, you'd have killed him."

"I shouldn't have said that to you. I didn't mean it."

"Of course you meant it, Dylan," Charlie said, shaking his head. "And he would have *deserved* it. The only difference is that if I'd been in your position that day, we wouldn't be having this conversation right now. Because Father would be dead, and I would be in an institution."

"No, Charlie, you're not like—"

Charlie spun around and cut him off sharply. "Don't! Don't you *dare* speak his name in this house. *Don't. You. Ever.*"

Dylan stood frozen, gazing with compassion into his brother's eyes until the fire waned. And when the last smoldering ember died out, Charlie released a soundless sigh and walked across the room to a small round table that stood in shadow. Centered on the glossy surface of the table was a black lacquered box with a discreet spring-loaded latch.

As he ran his fingertips along the sleek lid of the box, Charlie spoke in a serene tone. "Sometimes I come up here at night when everyone else is asleep, and I look down at this box and . . . " He trailed off, with a dreamy look in his eyes. Then his voice came back. " . . . and I just stand here, afraid to open it." He took a breath. "Other times, I open it without hesitation and just gaze at it, losing all sense of place and time." He took another breath, and his eyes suddenly looked haunted. "But I've never had the courage to put it on. Never once."

Charlie looked at Dylan. Then he turned back to the box, and with a subtle stroke of his forefinger along the little golden latch, he disengaged the lock. With smooth precision, the lid slid back and the front and side panels of the box collapsed outward, revealing the object within.

Instantly, a wave of icy tendrils raced over Dylan's body, but even as his breath caught in his throat, he managed to croak out a single question: "Where did you get that?"

"Sotheby's," Charlie said. "Grandmother bought it for

me. She didn't want to, but I convinced her that it would be better for us to have it than for it to fall into the hands of some bloodthirsty art collector. I had to promise her that I would destroy it, of course—and I will . . . eventually. But first I needed to . . . I needed to understand it." He shot a crooked half-smile at Dylan. "I know that may sound a little macabre to you, but I needed time to figure out its secrets . . . to look into its dark eyes and see what was going on inside that night . . . the night he put it on and became 'True Son, Second to the Last, Diviner of Secrets, Destroyer of Demagogues.'"

Outside, the moon broke from an errant patch of clouds, and misty streaks of light stabbed through the panoramic glass wall of the Solarium, illuminating the shiny black helmet-mask that sat on the table between Charlie and Dylan. The very same accoutrement that the terrorist known as True Son had worn on that fateful night nearly thirty-eight years ago. The night the President of the United States had made the critical mistake of underestimating his opponent, while the world watched in stunned disbelief.

Charlie squatted down now so that he was eye to eye with the black mask. "I've often wondered why he did it. What drove him to put on this mask and challenge a man with the power to crush him like a bug? Was it a misguided act of patriotism? Hubris? A sense of entitlement? A complete lack of respect for authority and utter disdain for the natural order of assimilation? Did he truly believe that he could destroy the movement of greatness by striking down its leader? Didn't he understand that there were more of us to come, that we would rise up to take our rightful place and complete the mission that our great-grandfather had started? Didn't he understand that resistance is futile?"

Charlie smiled sadly at the black mask, as one might smile at a child who has yet to learn life's cruel lessons.

Then he stood up straight and looked back to the glass

wall, beyond which lay the south lawn, where the labyrinthine hedge maze that had once swallowed him as a child now slumbered as if dreaming of his eventual return.

Dylan was still looking at the mask on the table when Charlie broke the silence.

"I see him," Charlie said. "Sometimes, in my dreams, I see him. Dressed in black, his mask and helmet gleaming under the dim lights . . . just as he was that night when he rose like a spectre to swallow Great-grandfather whole. Towering, majestic, all-encompassing. Walking the endless hallways, patiently seeking out his prey . . . " Charlie took a breath and let it out slowly. "And then he's gone, and all I see is you . . . and me . . . both of us moving in this eerie sort of slow-motion down those same halls he walked long before us. Not in D.C. but right here, inside The Winter White House—that's what they used to call this place: The Winter White House . . . and, trust me, Dylan, they *will* call it that again."

Charlie's eyes shined distantly with the diversion, and then he returned to his dream.

"I see us, you and I, Dylan," he said in a thick whisper. "In my dreams, I see us . . . one running, the other closing in. But my vision is cloudy, like it so often is in dreams, and I can never quite . . . I can never quite tell just which of us it is behind that mask."

They stood there in the darkened Solarium like figures in tableau: Charlie looking out at the night sky; Dylan gazing at the black mask on the table. There was nothing left to say.

Then out of the silence, Charlie's watch beeped, and in a chipper tone, he said, "Ah, it's nearly midnight. The guests should be gathering in the Gold Room. I'd better get going. I'll see you downstairs . . . unless you're planning on leaving before the surprise. If that is the case, please have the courtesy to tell me now."

Dylan shook his head and replied softly, "No, I'll stay."

"Good," Charlie said with a clipped nod. "I'll see you shortly then."

It wasn't until the sound of Charlie's footfalls had faded down the spiral staircase that Dylan realized something was wrong with his vision. At first, he thought he was dreaming and that he would wake up in his dorm room back at school to discover this odd encounter with Charlie had never happened. But as he swiped the tears from his eyes and saw that the mask on the table was really there, he knew that he wasn't dreaming.

He was wide awake, and things were far worse than he could have possibly imagined.

11

The Red Lounge was deserted by the time Dylan returned from the Solarium. A few guests were still outside on the patio, sharing a large hookah while another of Charlie's oldies from the Ed Sheeran Essentials Collection, a mellow tune entitled *Bloodstream*, drifted dreamily from the speakers, its hypnotic beat seemingly synchronized with the streaks of moonlight rippling along the surface of the pool.

Dylan looked to the sofa, where he and Lexie had left Hakhan and Akasha sleeping. Neither was there. He wondered if the bartender, James, had taken Hakhan back to the kennels. But James was nowhere to be found, either. Dylan considered asking the group on the patio if any of them had seen the large Shepalute, but judging by their current state, he was pretty sure the most he'd get would be a few lazy grins and dopey chuckles.

The corridor between the residence and the hotel was silent. For a moment Dylan felt lost. He briefly wondered if Lexie had gone back to the Atrium. Or maybe she'd gone upstairs to look for him. It was possible that while he was coming down in one elevator, she was going up in the other, and they passed each other without even knowing it.

His mind was still clouded with the strange conversation he'd had with Charlie up in the Solarium, and he couldn't get the image of that black mask with its shiny helmet out of his head.

I see us, you and I, Dylan . . . in my dream, I see us . . . but my vision is cloudy . . . and I can never quite tell just which of us it is behind that mask.

Charlie's voice was followed by Lexie's: *You're the good guy, and the good guy always stands up for the underdog.*

And then Charlie again: *It's a surprise. I've been working on it all month.*

And Lexie: *The love note . . . I didn't write it . . . but I wish I had.*

And finally Charlie once more: *It's nearly midnight. The guests should be gathering in the Gold Room.*

Dylan's heart thudded like the slow striking of a great hammer in his chest, and suddenly he felt an urgent need to find Lexie. Find her and leave this place before the stroke of midnight. Just get in his car with her and drive away, as fast and far as possible.

Technically, the Gold Room was located on the ground floor of the hotel, but its high ceiling and twin staircases swept up into the mezzanine, where the grand balcony offered a breathtaking view of the ballroom below, as well as the sprawling south lawn beyond the floor-to-ceiling mullioned windows. The room was packed with guests, all wearing New Year's masks—foxes, owls, bulls, boars, rabbits, gazelles, jesters, harlequins, pantelones, capitanos, venetians—all waiting for the countdown to begin.

Dylan stood in the ornate archway for a moment, searching the hall for Lexie. Then he began to make his way through the crowd, bumping shoulders along the way. Despite the accelerated beating of his heart, he held himself tightly in check. He needed to find Lexie, and he wasn't going to do that by panicking. But the deeper he got into the room, the faster and stronger his heart seemed to beat, as if it were trying to pound a hole straight through his chest.

He had searched the sea of masks, confident that he would recognize Lexie's stunning green eyes, even at a glance. But suddenly he wasn't so sure anymore, and as the countdown began, he started pulling up masks on each girl he encountered. But none of them were Lexie.

In his mind, he could hear the voice from that fateful night. Though it had happened long before he was born, the old broadcast from the Oval Office could still be found on the internet, and Dylan had watched every moment of it: the night his great-grandfather had been dismantled on live television by a brilliant young man in the same mask that now sat on the table up in the Solarium. And as he continued to search for Lexie in the crowded ballroom, the voice of that young man in the mask rang inside his head: *I am True Son, Second to the Last, Destroyer of Demagogs.*

And then Charlie's voice, cold and deadly: *Don't you speak his name in this house. Don't. You. Ever.*

Dylan stopped suddenly and looked up at the huge clock suspended above the crowd at the center of the Gold Room. In seconds it would be midnight, and he was all alone in this crowded hall.

He closed his eyes and heard Lexie's voice again: *I didn't write it . . . but I wish I had.* And at that moment—just before the stroke of midnight—he knew one thing with certainty: He wished she had, too.

He felt a hand tapping on his shoulder as the crowd counted down in unison: FIVE . . . FOUR . . . THREE . . . TWO . . .

He turned to see Lexie smiling at him, and as the clock struck midnight, she kissed him, and he closed his eyes and kissed her back.

When their lips parted, she said, "I told you I'd find you."

Dylan nodded, his forehead touching hers, his eyes still closed.

Lexie laughed, but it wasn't her usual laugh. "Jesus, you're trembling. Are you all right?"

Dylan nodded again, this time looking at her. "Yeah."

She smiled, but there was a concern in her eyes. She was about to say something when Charlie suddenly appeared. She gave him a big hug and several kisses on the cheek. "Happy New Year, Charlie."

"All right then," Charlie said with a chuckle. "Happy New Year to you too, Lexie."

When Lexie finally released him, Charlie looked at Dylan. The brothers both smiled, but neither seemed to know what to do or say. For a moment, they were caught in that clumsy pantomime between a hug, a handshake or a simple nod of acknowledgment.

Charlie broke the awkward moment with a clipped nod and extended his hand. "I suppose a handshake should suffice."

Dylan smiled and shook his brother's hand, but he didn't let go when Charlie released his grip. He just looked into Charlie's eyes.

"OK, then," Charlie said with a short laugh. He was about to add "Happy New Year" when Dylan pulled him into an embrace.

A surprised laugh escaped Charlie, and when his brother's cheek brushed against his, he laughed again and said, "You need a shave, Dylan." The embrace tightened, and Charlie smiled and said, "You're going to crush me, Dylan."

But Dylan just held him tighter. Charlie was about to laugh again—he didn't know what else to do—but then something unexpected happened. A soft sound escaped Dylan, and suddenly the tide within Charlie shifted.

And then he was hugging Dylan back and trying to cover the tremor in his voice. "Hey, it's OK. Everything's OK, right? We're here, right? We made it. Another year." His voice caught in his throat, and he pushed back against the shifting tide. "No more fighting, OK? I don't want to fight anymore . . . I won't fight anymore, OK?"

When Dylan released the embrace, Charlie was suddenly afraid to let go. He didn't know if he could take seeing Dylan cry. Not now. Not when all he had planned for over the past month was so close to fruition.

But when they parted, Dylan wasn't crying. His eyes were glassy, but he wasn't crying. He even pushed a smile to show Charlie that there were no hard feelings over their dustup at Cambridge back in November.

"This is going to be a good year," Charlie said, his eyes alight with sudden vigor. "Best year ever. We're going to put the past behind us and lean forward." He paused briefly and then added, "And after tonight we'll be able to do just that."

Dylan's smile faltered, and his eyes narrowed in confusion, even as Charlie beamed at him with delight. Then before Dylan could ask Charlie what he was up to, the sea of guests parted as the lights dimmed and the platform between the two curving grand staircases rose from the floor in dramatic fashion. Under the warm glow of an overhead spotlight, stood an Imperial Bösendorfer grand piano, with a double-wide cushioned bench.

At the sight of the piano, Dylan's faltering smile curled into a crooked grin. "This is your big surprise?"

"You can't deny me," Charlie said. "Not on my New Year's wish."

Dylan shook his head, smiling dubiously now. "I haven't played in years, Charlie."

"You never forget how to play, Dylan. It's in our blood. I'll be right there with you. If we go down, we go down together."

Dylan was still shaking his head and looking at the piano as if it were a slumbering animal best left undisturbed when Lexie said, "I didn't know you played."

"If you want to call it that," Dylan responded in self-effacing sarcasm.

"He's being modest," Charlie said. "He taught me everything I know. We played to a sold-out crowd at the Geffen Hall when I was eleven and he was fifteen."

"We played at the Geffen Hall because Morgana commissioned the place for a fundraiser. They didn't come to see us."

"But they *loved* us," Charlie persisted. "We brought down the house!"

Dylan's lips parted, but before he could protest any further, Lexie said, "Oh, you have to play. Do it for me. *Please.*"

Looking into her impossibly beautiful eyes, Dylan couldn't say no. But as he followed Charlie up the steps and onto the platform, he couldn't shake the feeling that there was more to Charlie's surprise than this impromptu performance. Dylan knew his younger brother better than anyone, and with Charlie, things were rarely as simple as they appeared to be on the surface. Indeed they were often infinitely more complex.

At the piano, Charlie asked Dylan which he would prefer, the upper or lower register, and Dylan's heart swelled because that had been his line when they were younger. From a very young age, Charlie had been fascinated by the fluid movement of Dylan's fingers over the keys. He would sit for hours watching Dylan play, his own fingers moving over the surface of the coffee table or the floor, mimicking the mystifying ballet of those elegant fingers as they drew sounds from the piano that swept through his little body with the force of a rolling wave, threatening to take him under and drown him. Sometimes while he lay in bed, unable to sleep, the notes of Chopin's *Ballade No. 1 in G minor,*

Op 23 or *Waltz No. 3 in A Minor, Op. 34, No. 2* would come at him in the darkness with such force that he could scarcely breathe. Like velvet daggers, each keystroke would stab at him, slice by slice, tearing their way into his soul until all he wanted, all he could see was himself seated on that bench next to his older brother, commanding those keys to show him that same respect.

"Depends," Dylan said now with a wink. "What do you want to play?"

"The Prokofiev?" Charlie posed with a grin. He was referring to *Concerto No. 2*, one of the top ten most difficult piano pieces to play, and Dylan rolled his eyes as expected.

"Yeah, try again."

Charlie considered. *"Nocturne in C-Sharp Minor?"*

It was the first piece Charlie had mastered. He had been six at the time, and he'd played it while sitting on Dylan's lap. It was his proudest moment because when he'd finished there were tears in his older brother's eyes.

"You take the upper," Dylan said, and they sat down, Dylan on the left, and Charlie on the right.

As the chords filled the hall, Lexie stood mesmerized. She had never seen anything like it: two boys, seemingly opposite in every conceivable respect but this one. The left hand of the older boy perfectly in sync with the right hand of the younger, as if both were the extensions of a single entity.

Though she had shared the most intimate physical act possible with one of them, her bond with the other ran deeper than mere friendship, and as the music spilled from the piano, Lexie felt torn because, until this very moment, she hadn't believed it possible to fall in love with two people at the same time.

When the last note of the Nocturne was struck and the applause rang out, Charlie smiled at Dylan and queried, "Encore?"

Dylan looked into Charlie's eyes as the applause continued and said, "Tell me what this is all about, Charlie."

"I don't know what you mean, Dylan."

"Sure you do." It didn't come out sarcastically, or com-
batively. He didn't want to start another fight; he just wanted
the truth.

Charlie laughed. "What are you talking about?"

Dylan opened his mouth to tell Charlie exactly what he
was talking about, but just then the crowd got louder, chanting, "Encore! Encore!"

"You want to know what this is about?" Charlie asked.
"It's about this. Just this. This single moment. You and me.
One last night."

Dylan gazed at his brother, searching his eyes, as the
crowd continued to chant, "Encore! Encore!"

Charlie smiled as he reached across Dylan's chest and
positioned his elegant fingers above the lower register of the
keyboard.

His hand hovered there for but a moment, like a diver
at the edge of a cliff.

Then he began to play two familiar notes, up and down,
up and down, like the rhythm of a skipping rope, waiting
for Dylan to jump in. His smile deepened as if daring Dylan
to resist the temptation. "Come on, Dylan," he coaxed. "You
know this one."

Dylan did know it. It was the theme to an old movie
called *The Usual Suspects*—the same piece of music that,
according to legend, had been played on the grand piano
in the Cross Hall of the White House by their granduncles,
Dane and Barret Kingley, the night their great-grandfather
had gone mano a mano on live TV with the masked terrorist
known as True Son.

Dylan's thoughts shifted to the black mask up in the
Solarium—the mask that True Son had worn on that fateful
night—and he looked at his younger brother with scarcely

veiled desperation and whispered, "You're not like him, Charlie."

Still smiling that pleasant smile, Charlie replied, "I know I'm not like him, Dylan." He paused briefly and then added deliberately, "But I'm worried that *you* might be."

Charlie continued to play the two-note riff as he gazed into Dylan's eyes, unwaveringly. And when he nodded to the lower end of the piano, Dylan's fingers slipped into place and took over as Charlie retracted his left hand and began to play the upper register with his right hand.

What happened next was both dreamlike and frighteningly real at once. As the haunting music filled the hall, a tall figure in a tuxedo and papier-mâché mask in the form of a cunning wolf approached Lexie and spoke into her ear. Dylan continued to play as he watched Lexie make her way toward the exit with the tall figure in the wolf mask.

Charlie felt Dylan tensing beside him and placed his left hand on Dylan's knee. "Relax, Dylan," he said, softly. "It's part of the surprise. Lexie knows that. Everything is fine. It's all going according to plan."

Dylan watched as Lexie disappeared through the darkened archway at the east end of the Gold Room, and even though every instinct in his body cried out for him to get up and follow her, he continued to play right along with Charlie.

"Don't blame her, Dylan. I made her promise not to tell you. She can't resist when I show her my puppy eyes." He made his puppy eyes at Dylan. "She thinks she's in love with me—and I suspect that some part of her actually is. But whatever the reason, she's never been able to resist me. And, truthfully, neither have you, Dylan."

They continued to play in silence, the left hand of the older brother moving over the lower register of the keyboard, striking each note in perfect synchronization with the right hand of the younger. But Dylan was no longer concentrating on the music. His gaze had drifted to the crowd, where other masked figures in tuxedos suddenly appeared from the shadows and, like a garrison of exotic deadly animals, took positions at each of the exits.

Applause exploded on the final note, and Dylan tensed. "What is this, Charlie?"

"I already told you, silly," Charlie said. "It's a surprise. Just relax. You're going to like it."

The blood coursed rapidly through Dylan's veins now as he gazed at his younger brother, searching his eyes for a sign of the sweet boy who had once sat on his lap and played Chopin's *Nocturne in C-Sharp Minor* without missing a single note.

Charlie gazed back at him with that eerily pleasant expression. Then he leaned in close, placing a cool hand on the back of Dylan's neck, and with his lips almost touching Dylan's ear, he whispered, "You smell like sex, Dylan. Next time you fuck one of my friends, have the decency to wash up after. We're not savages. We are the chosen ones."

He withdrew and looked into Dylan's eyes, hard, fierce, proud. And then his pleasant smile returned, as if he'd donned an impenetrable mask.

12

Dylan sat still as Charlie rose from the bench and stepped away from the piano to address his guests. He raised his hands to silence the applause and said, "Thank you. You're very kind. And now if you will all direct your attention to the screens you see descending around the room, as promised, I have a little surprise to ring in the New Year . . ."

On cue, six massive TV screens descended from the ceiling, each offering a different view of the hedge maze outside. A wave of excitement passed through the crowd, but Dylan, who knew Charlie better than any of them, felt a sudden chill.

"Although," Charlie went on, "I'm not sure how much of a surprise it actually is, since I've heard through the grapevine that many of you have been placing wagers on the outcome."

A ripple of laughter passed through the masked guests around the hall, and Charlie smiled as if to say *I won't tell if you won't tell.*

"But for those who don't know what the surprise is," Charlie continued. "My big brother Dylan, whom I believe most of you know—" An explosion of cheers and applause came from the crowd, and Charlie winked at Dylan the way one might wink at a celebrity before turning back to the crowd. "Popular guy, very popular—especially with the ladies . . . " The girls screamed with delight. " . . . and, let's be PC here, he's drawn his fair share of glances from some of the guys, as well . . . " Low laughter, peppered with catcalling and whistling came from Dylan's former teammates. "But he's taken," Charlie cautioned with a grin, "so, all of you, keep your hands to yourselves." A wave of mock groans—once again, mostly from Dylan's soccer buddies— passed through the Gold Room. "I'm not going to name names," Charlie called out, "except for you, Grach, because we all know what a scandalous rogue you are."

The crowd laughed, and Xander Grach let out a wolf cry that echoed around the hall. Still sitting at the piano, Dylan braced himself as his heart drummed a slow, driving beat in his chest.

"So," Charlie said as the laughter died down, "my big brother Dylan has agreed to take up the New Year's challenge. For those of you who are unfamiliar with this challenge, it's something we used to do every year, Dylan and I, back when we were kids . . . "

The chill that Dylan had felt racing his spine a moment ago now spread out over his entire body, and his heartbeat accelerated. The New Year's challenge was sort of like an Easter egg hunt, but instead of hunting for hidden eggs, you searched for hidden items of value. Charlie had come up with the challenge the winter after his spooky night in the hedge maze. The rules were simple: he and Dylan would raid each other's rooms for three items the other valued most, and separately they would hide the items in the maze. Then shortly after midnight, while the adults were partying in the packed Gold Room, the two boys would sneak out-side and race through the maze on their quest to find the hidden treasures, and the first to recover all three of his items was the winner.

Dylan couldn't remember the last time he'd even thought about the challenge. They hadn't done it in years—not since Charlie had graduated from primary school to middle school. Dylan had assumed that Charlie had forgot-ten about it; packed it away with all the other childish things he'd pushed to the back of his mental closet upon reaching what he considered to be adulthood at the age of thirteen.

But Charlie hadn't forgotten the New Year's challenge.

And he hadn't forgotten the argument they'd had out-side the Science Center at Harvard back in November, either. Indeed the latter had been his sole reason for inviting Dylan to this party, where he was about to resurrect their child-hood game before a live audience.

Except, this time, the challenge would be different.

This time, only *one* of them would be entering the maze in search of those three items of value. And judging by the Machiavellian gleam in Charlie's eyes, Dylan was fairly certain the stakes would be higher than his prized hockey stick or favorite pair of roller blades. The only question was how *much* higher? How far was Charlie willing to take this game? What was waiting for Dylan inside the hedge maze?

The answer to all three questions came like a gut punch that sucked the breath out of Dylan and left him stunned.

"Three clues for Dylan," Charlie announced to the crowd as a masked figure in evening dress handed him a velvet sack. "Three clues that only he will understand—and that will lead him to those three most prized items hidden in the maze. And the first clue is . . . "

With a flourish, Charlie reached into the velvet sack and produced the first clue. And at once, a rush of blood crashed at Dylan's temples.

"A bundle of cash," Charlie called out with mock surprise. "Five thousand dollars, crisp and fresh, straight from the cashier's cage!"

The crowd reacted with awe and intrigue and applause as Charlie set the bundle of cash on the piano.

As Dylan gazed at the cash he'd won at his father's casino a few nights back, Charlie leaned in and said softly, "Imagine Gerald's surprise when he found this in the locker of one of our youngest valets. Such a sweet kid. Just received a promotion too. But then, you never can tell with the hired help, can you?"

Dylan turned to his brother and pierced him with a hard look. Charlie raised a finger to his lips and dropped a conspiratorial wink.

"I told Gerald not to involve the police. Surely it must be a misunderstanding. I told him that you would be able to clear up the whole matter. After all, Beto is like the younger brother you always wanted but were denied—handsome, athletic, normal, so very like you, Dylan. I'm certain you'll be able to find your lost *hermano* and help him out of this mess he's gotten himself into before it's too late. He's counting on you, Dylan. Don't let him down."

Charlie turned back to the crowd just as the applause was dying out. "And for the second clue, we have . . . " He reached into the velvet sack again and produced a rawhide dog bone. "Dylan . . . " he called out with a sly grin, playing more to the crowd than to his brother, "is there something you want to tell us? Some . . . fetish you've been hiding?"

The crowd roared with laughter. As Charlie set the large bone on the piano beside the bundle of cash, Dylan's mind flashed on the empty sofa in the Red Lounge where he and Lexie had left Hakhan and Akasha sleeping, and his pulse quickened again.

"And now for the final clue . . . "

Charlie reached into the sack one last time, but for Dylan, there was no suspense. He already knew what the third "item of value" hidden in the maze was. He closed his eyes, forcing himself to breathe while in his mind, he replayed the moment during his and Charlie's performance when Lexie was called away by the tall figure in the wolf mask. Silently, he cursed himself for not getting up and putting a stop to this whole thing right then and there.

A curious murmur passed through the crowd, and Dylan opened his eyes as Charlie announced, "It's a note. Written on pink paper . . . and folded with such care. Could it be a love note? From a secret admirer, perhaps?"

The crowd played along, oohing and aahing while Dylan sat frozen, staring at the folded sheet of paper held up between Charlie's elegant fingers.

It was a love note—the very same that Dylan had found in his locker back in his senior year of high school, the one that he'd thought Lexie had written. He remembered taking it home with him that day and reading it in his room. But sometime after, it had vanished, and this was the first he'd seen it since.

It wasn't difficult to imagine Charlie finding the note while looking for something in his room—Charlie often borrowed things from Dylan's room without asking, and Dylan never minded. But for Charlie to have taken this note and kept it all these years . . . it didn't make sense. What possible fascination or meaning could a love note written to Dylan by an anonymous girl at his high school have held for Charlie?

And more importantly, why would Charlie connect the note with Lexie?

Dylan was still puzzling over this when Charlie called out dramatically, "So, Dylan, are you ready to take up the challenge?"

The crowd roared.

Dylan stood and, facing Charlie, said softly. "You've made your point. You want my attention, I'll give it to you. I'll listen to whatever you have to say."

121

"Oh, Dylan," Charlie said with a smile, "we're past all that. It's time for the challenge now. You don't want to disappoint our guests."

"Call it off," Dylan said. "Whatever this is, call it off, and I'll listen to you."

Charlie's smile became dreamily pleasant. "But what good will it do for you to listen if the outcome will be the same? You've already made your decision to leave without consulting me. Nothing I could say will change that, right?" He put a hand on Dylan's shoulder and squeezed. "Freedom comes with a price, Dylan. If the hero wants to cross the bridge, he has to pay the troll his due."

Charlie released his grasp on Dylan's shoulder, but before he could retract his hand, Dylan reached across his chest and pinned Charlie's hand down to his shoulder in a firm grip. It wasn't painful, but it stunned the smile off of Charlie's face and forced him to meet Dylan's gaze.

"It's not too late to stop it, Charlie."

Charlie hesitated, a brief flicker in his eyes. Then, without malice, he said softly, "I'm afraid it is. I couldn't stop it now if I wanted to. You're the only one who can do that, Dylan."

They stood there like statues as the crowd took up the chant: "Dylan, Dylan, Dylan . . . "

And then Charlie smiled again and said, "Relax. Have fun. It's just a party game. And you're the guest of honor." His hand slipped from under Dylan's, and he turned back to the chanting crowd and called out, "Are you ready?"

The response was a resounding round of applause and cheers.

"All right then," Charlie called out. "Let's do this!" And even louder, he commanded, "Reset the clock!"

On the screen at the center of the hall, a large digital clock appeared: 30:00.

"Dylan," Charlie called out, "you have thirty minutes to find and reclaim all three items of value!"

At once, two masked figures stepped up on either side of Dylan as he gazed up at the clock on the center screen, his body tense, his throat too dry to swallow. Before they guided Dylan out of the hall and down to the north entrance of the hedge maze outside, Charlie turned to his brother and strapped a watch around his wrist. He pressed a small button on the side, and the glass face of the watch glowed into life, displaying the same digits as the big clock on the center screen. With a reassuring look, Charlie said, "Don't worry. The countdown won't begin until you enter the maze."

13

The temperature outside had dropped considerably, and a cool breeze washed over Dylan's face as he passed under the arched bough at the north end of the maze. The hedges loomed tall on either side of him. The only light came from the misty moon, passing through a bank of clouds in the dark sky above. Once Dylan entered the maze proper, the watch strapped to his wrist glowed into life. He looked down immediately and saw that the countdown had begun: 29:59:33, 29:58:46, 29:57:22 . . .

It was the standard time that he and Charlie had set for the game back when they were kids. But they weren't kids anymore, and this wasn't a game—at least not in the sense that it had been on all those New Year's Eves past. The look in Charlie's eyes just before Dylan had been escorted out of the Gold Room had told Dylan that much. But there were also the strange things Charlie had spoken of up in the Solarium.

Sometimes I come up here at night when everyone else is asleep, and I look down at this box . . .

Sometimes in my dreams, I see him. Dressed in black, his mask and helmet gleaming under the dim lights . . . just as he was that night when he rose like a spectre to swallow Great-grandfather whole.

I see us, you and I, Dylan . . . in my dreams, I see us . . . one running, the other closing in . . .

And all the while that black mask had sat there on the table between them, as if life still breathed within it—as if the tormented soul who had once stared down the most powerful man in the world through those dark glass eyes was watching them from beyond the grave, waiting to see which would take up the mantle.

That alone had given Dylan more than enough cause for alarm. And now as the milliseconds rapidly dwindled, he looked away from the wristwatch and focused on the challenge.

The clues had been presented in a specific order—the cash that he'd given to Beto, the rawhide dog bone, the love note—and, knowing Charlie, Dylan was certain this had not been done by chance. Any plan of Charlie's would be meticulously thought out, down to the last detail, well before being set into motion. And any deviation from this plan by Dylan would be met with what Charlie would refer to as "corrective action."

If Dylan wanted to win, he would have to do so honorably. He couldn't just call out into the darkness, wait for a response and then track the prizes by the sounds of their voices (Hakhan would be the easiest to find because once he heard Dylan's voice, he wouldn't stop barking until Dylan found him). But that would be cheating, and Charlie did not tolerate cheating. The first New Year's they'd done the challenge, Dylan had deliberately slowed his pace so that Charlie would find his three items first and emerge the winner (it was, after all, Charlie's game, and Dylan hadn't wanted to beat his younger brother at any challenge, least of all one the kid had invented). But even at the age of seven-going-on-eight, Charlie had razor-sharp senses and knew that Dylan had let him win.

"You can't cheat, Dylan," Charlie had said, though not with anger, or even disappointment. He'd said it with a calm expression and a maturity well beyond his years. "There's no point in playing if you cheat—even if it's for a good reason." (Years later, during one of their more passionate disagreements over their great-grandfather's dubious election to the presidency, Dylan would remember this firm stance on the issue of cheating, but he would resist the urge to use his younger brother's own words against him.)

To beat Charlie, Dylan would have to rely solely upon his wits and skill. And he would have to do it on the terms that Charlie had once believed in with all his heart.

But beating Charlie wasn't what concerned Dylan. If this were just a game, Dylan would gladly throw it and bow to his kid brother in front of all of their schoolmates. If it would help Charlie let go of the anger he still harbored over Dylan's "betrayal" of the family, Dylan would readily accept defeat and acknowledge Charlie's superior gamesmanship.

But this wasn't a game. It was a challenge. A challenge which Dylan was now convinced would have far-reaching consequences that even Charlie could not comprehend—at least not in his present state of silent fury and fixation—and one that could have dire consequences for the three unwitting participants waiting out there in the darkness for Dylan to find them.

Thinking about it from this angle made Dylan feel a bit foolish. Surely Charlie would never do anything to harm an innocent bystander. It was true that he had their father's temper, and he certainly had their grandmother's penchant for delayed retribution. But Charlie was meticulous to a fault, and, at least to the best of Dylan's recollection, he had never once deviated from the target of his ire.

But what if, in Charlie's reckoning, the innocent bystanders weren't entirely innocent?

In a flash, Dylan could hear Charlie's voice, slicing through his consciousness like a razor . . .

After all, Beto is like the younger brother you always wanted . . . so very like you, Dylan . . . I'm certain you'll be able to find your lost hermano and help him out of this mess he's gotten himself into before it's too late.

We have three others from Hakhan's litter—all excellent guard dogs and very obedient. But, as you can see, Dylan spoiled this one, and now he's practically useless for his purpose.

You smell like sex, Dylan. Next time you fuck one of my friends, have the decency to wash up after.

With three minutes on the clock expired and twenty-seven left, Dylan headed into the darkness in search of the three souls hidden in the depths of the maze.

While the guests in the Gold Room watched Dylan's progress on the suspended TV screens, Charlie receded into the shadows behind the grand piano and slipped out of the hall, unnoticed.

His gait was purposeful but not rushed as he made his way down the glass corridor toward the bank of elevators. He didn't check his watch while waiting for the elevator; he didn't need too. He'd rehearsed the whole thing multiple times until he had every move down to the second, with more than enough time to spare.

On the ride to the upstairs residence, a soft beep emitted from his pocket, and he took out his phone. A crisp image of the maze outside was displayed on the small screen, and Charlie smiled thinly at the simplicity of dealing with a thoroughly predictable opponent.

Dylan had reached the first marker right on schedule and had found the first clue: a sneaker, its toe pointed at the pathway to the left—the mate for this shoe would be found nine meters down the adjoining path, pointing the way to the next marker. Charlie hadn't been altogether sure his cagey older brother would take the bait, so he'd installed several "motivators" along the way.

Using the touchpad on his phone's screen, Charlie triggered one of these motivators now, and instantly, a thin branch, trimmed to a fine switch, sprang out from the lush green wall of the maze with deadly speed just as Dylan made a move toward the pathway to the left.

As expected, his older brother's reflexes were exceptional. Dylan ducked the whipping branch in the nick of time, sparing himself a nasty lash across the cheek, possibly even a laceration to the eye.

The expression on his face as he looked up at the extended branch was priceless. The tightened jaw, the flaring nostrils, the hard, almost indignant sheen in the eyes. Cliché, yes, but then Dylan was really no different than the myriad handsome heroes in the movies who thought they could muscle their way to a victory over an intellectually superior adversary. Lombard, the smugly handsome prick in *And Then There Were None*—the old movie he and Dylan had watched as kids—had believed he could muscle his way through it. But in the end, he'd been beaten by a girl. Of course, the girl got what was coming to her as well—justice had been served all around in that classic movie, and nobody came out alive.

Charlie smiled his razor-thin smile as the elevator doors opened onto the residence floor, while on his phone's little screen, Dylan lifted himself from the grass and proceeded in the very direction that the booby-trapped branch had attempted to dissuade him from traveling.

Yes, Charlie thought, Dylan was just like all those arrogant heroes in movies, stubbornly pressing on, not in spite of the warning but in willful defiance of it.

Charlie dropped his phone back into his pocket as he stepped from the elevator and headed down the hall, toward the room his two eldest brothers referred to as "The Armory."

. . .

The trail of clues, which had started with the single sneaker pointing the way from the first marker, continued along the paths with other articles of clothing: a pair of socks, each marking a different turn into the maze; a long-sleeved shirt hanging from a branch; a white tank top at the base of a stone birdbath; and finally, a pair of blue jeans, both legs pointed toward a shadowy path that led to a dead end. Dylan knew this because it had been his favorite place in the maze back when he was a kid—a cozy little alcove where he had often gone to escape the family. Charlie had dubbed it their "quiet place" after he'd discovered Dylan on the wooden bench inside with a copy of *Treasure Island* one sunny afternoon. Instead of asking Dylan to read aloud, Charlie had just climbed into his brother's lap and read silently along with him. After that day, it had become an unspoken rule that the "quite place" was for reading only; once inside, they would curl up on the bench with a book, Charlie in Dylan's lap, the back of his head resting comfortably against Dylan's chest, both of them silent and focused on the book; though Dylan was a faster reader, he always waited patiently for Charlie's small hand to tap his leg, indicating that it was time to turn the page.

Looking down the darkened path now, Dylan steeled himself against the sudden and painful wave of nostalgia and forced himself to focus. Could it really be this easy? Could this trail of clothing, laid out like breadcrumbs in a fable, lead him straight to the prize? It just didn't seem like Charlie at all. It was too simple. Too straightforward. Too anticlimactic. With Charlie, there was always a twist. No reward was given for simply following instructions; if you wanted his offering, you had to prove yourself worthy.

Dylan took a breath, preparing himself for the inevitable twist before heading down the path toward the "quiet place" at the end.

Misty streaks of moonlight spilled into the alcove at a slanted angle, and Dylan halted at the sight before him. It wasn't the twist he'd expected, but it certainly was shocking.

Beto sat on the bench, clad only in his boxer shorts, his head lolling forward so that Dylan couldn't see his face. His feet were planted on the grass and his arms hung limp at his sides. He was either unconscious or semiconscious, and the only thing keeping him from falling forward and flat on his face was the coil of white nylon rope lashed around his upper body and tied off to the backrest of the bench.

When Dylan's paralysis broke, he stepped forward, and instantaneously a red light flashed on his periphery. His eyes darted in the direction of the flashing light, and his heart skipped a beat. Here was Charlie's twist, and it was blood-chilling.

At the top of the tall hedge wall, one of the crossbows from the Armory was rigged and pointed at Beto. The red dot indicator flashed on the device affixed to the crossbow. And a digital clock started counting down from thirty seconds. There was no way to reach the crossbow and divert its trajectory; it was far too high.

Dylan tore his gaze from the digital clock and raced to Beto. He stared at the complicated configuration of knots for an agonizing series of seconds, trying to find the one that would release Beto. But there didn't seem to be an end to the knots. They just went on and on, twisting and turning into each other.

Dylan was about to give up on the knots and attempt to lift and move the bench with Beto on it when he noticed the message written on Beto's bare stomach in greasepaint: *Why not use the knife?*

Dylan looked around wildly. And there it was: a hunting knife from the Armory, stabbed into the armrest at one end of the bench. He lunged for the haft of the knife and yanked it from the armrest. Not daring to look around at the counter on the crossbow, he immediately set to work cutting through the thick knots of the rope.

When he finally cut through the first trail of rope attached to the bench, he knew that he'd never get through the other in time. But it didn't matter. With the one side free, he was able to shift Beto's body sideways and just out of range a split second before the clock ran out.

The arrow flew like a bullet—narrowly missing Dylan's right ear—and pierced the backrest of the bench with deadly force.

Dylan gazed at the arrow, trying to gauge whether it had landed on the mark or just to the left of where Beto had been sitting. Either way, it had been close enough to confirm his worst fear: Charlie's New Year's challenge was indeed far more than a game.

He cut Beto free with the knife and then tried to wake him. Beto opened his eyes briefly and smiled a sad drunken smile. Dylan could smell the tequila on his breath.

"I'm sorry," Beto slurred in Spanish. "They made me . . . they said I had to be initiated . . . are you mad at me?"

Dylan shook his head, and he touched Beto's hair the way he used to touch Charlie's hair when Charlie was little. Tears suddenly filled Beto's eyes.

"My mom can't see me like this, hermano . . . I can't have her see me like this . . . "

"She's not gonna see you like this. I promise."

"I'm so messed up . . . I don't know why I let them . . . I should have said no . . . I'm sorry . . . I'm . . . "

Beto's voice trailed off in an incoherent mumble as he curled into a ball and drifted back to sleep.

Dylan wanted to backtrack to collect Beto's clothes, but with less than twenty minutes left on the clock, there wasn't enough time. So he took off his jacket and draped it over Beto, who curled into a tighter ball but did not stir.

Before he left the alcove, Dylan used the hunting knife to cut a short strip from the coil of the nylon rope that had been wrapped around Beto's upper body and tucked it into his pocket.

Charlie stood in the shadows of the atrium now, gazing down at the helmet with its protruding mask and shiny black eyes, wondering if this was what it was like for True Son the last time he'd donned his disguise and stepped before the camera to face down his enemy in the grand finale. Had he feared the end? Or had he embraced it with all his heart?

Charlie had watched the footage of that final encounter between True Son and the President over and over, studying every movement, memorizing every word, every song that True Son had carefully selected and played right on cue. It had been a masterful performance, flawlessly staged and executed—even Charlie's great-grandfather, the President himself, had been in awe of his opponent's showmanship.

But still, Charlie wondered what it had been like for True Son. Beneath the façade. Inside the mask. What had he felt? Fear? Pain? A sense of release? Immortality? Surely, he had known that he would live on in infamy, cast in the annals of history, never to be forgotten. A hero to some, a villain to others, but never to be forgotten.

Was it martyrdom he'd sought? Or had it simply been a performance for an audience of one? How desperate would you have to be to sacrifice everything you had or ever would have just to be seen by one person? Could it possibly have been that simple? The message his followers had displayed as they'd stood on the grounds of the Capitol on that bitterly cold night seemed to have suggested as much. But could it really have been as simple as that? Had the young man known as True Son brought the nation—the entire world— to a grinding halt with a mere cry for attention?

Charlie looked down at his phone's screen, where Dylan was presently searching the maze for his second prize. An unexpected wave of compassion flitted across Charlie's eyes as he watched his older brother, while in the very same moment, his lips pressed together in a cruel hard line, and he thought, perhaps nothing had been going through True Son's mind at the end. Perhaps it had been far too late for second thoughts.

Charlie looked at the mask and then back at his phone. Dylan's progress was getting him closer but not nearly fast enough. So with a deft thumb-stroke, Charlie gave his older brother a nudge in the right direction.

It was, after all, too late for second thoughts.

Dylan halted in his tracks and listened.

Soft music rose in the distance. Tentative bows quavering over the high strings of violins—the unmistakable sound of impending dread just before the hero discovers something grisly beyond the closed door in a horror movie.

Dylan remembered Charlie's childhood penchant for scary movies—*They should do one where he gets them all . . . where there's nobody left at the end, you know?*—and he steeled his nerves, trying to convince himself that this was only a game, that Charlie would never deliberately harm anyone.

The crossbow back in the alcove hadn't been aimed at Beto. The arrow had struck the bench beside him. Charlie would never have harmed Beto. It was just a game to him. His only desire was to get Dylan's attention.

The image of the two of them standing outside the Science Center in Cambridge the day before the election surfaced in Dylan's mind: Charlie with his hands clenched into white-knuckled fists, his gaze hard and icy.

I'm not crazy.

I'm not saying you're crazy, Charlie. I'm saying that what you said is crazy.

But suddenly Dylan wasn't so sure about his brother's mental stability. Thinking back on that bright and chilly day, he recalled the look in Charlie's eyes—an odd look that didn't jibe with the little boy he'd laughed and played with and held in his arms until all the bad feelings had gone away. There was pain and bitterness in this older version of his kid brother that no amount of soothing could wash away.

Dylan was pulled from his thoughts by a dramatic shift in the music. Deep, foreboding chords, struck on the lower register of a piano, rose in the distance now, and instantly Dylan turned his gaze toward the southwest corner of the maze. His first thought was that it might be a diversionary tactic, but he dismissed this at once. Charlie's quixotic partiality for intrigue and mystery notwithstanding, he was scrupulously pragmatic and had a low tolerance for convolution and misdirection. In Charlie's opinion, the truly great mysteries always ended with you shaking your head in wonder that you didn't recognize the killer from the very start; anything less was a cheat.

Despite the twisting configuration of the maze, it took less than two minutes to track the music to its source. As Dylan drew closer, the eerie chords filled his senses with dread, not only for their depth and intensity but, moreover, for the fact that he recognized every note.

It was the same music that had been playing that night nearly forty years ago when his great-grandfather entered the Oval Office for his first encounter via satellite with the masked terrorist known as True Son.

The Red Capes Are Coming, a piece from the music score of an old movie entitled *Batman v Superman: Dawn of Justice.* Though the movie had long been forgotten, the music True Son had co-opted from it to underscore his dramatic entrance remained in the top one hundred downloads to this very day.

As the music swelled, Dylan became aware of another

sound—soft yet distinct: a mournful whine that he would have recognized anywhere. And suddenly, he was running, racing along the pathways and bends toward the source of that pitiful whine.

Dylan rounded the last corner and came to an abrupt stop, his gaze fixed on the rounded enclosure at the end of the path. Through the entryway, he could see Hakhan. The dog lay flat on his belly, his chin resting on his outstretched paws, his eyes darting around tentatively as the eerie music drifted down from the speakers mounted high on the hedge walls. The leather muzzle strapped around Hakhan's snout and head prevented him from barking, but he continued to emit the low, pitiful whine that had brought Dylan running.

The sight of the dog hunkered down on the dewy grass caused Dylan's gut to twist and his jaw to clench. He was less than nine meters away and ready to make the dash when Hakhan saw him. At once, the whining ceased, and Hakhan's ears shot up. Dylan's heart stopped cold because he knew what was going to happen next, and he was powerless to prevent it. His first instinct was to bolt down the path, but he knew he would never bridge the distance in time so instead, he raised a cautioning hand.

Hakhan's head was raised, but he was still on his belly, his eyes focused on Dylan, his huge tail thumping the grass. A low, anticipatory whine escaped him, but he remained still . . . even when Dylan took his first cautious step toward him.

"Easy," Dylan said, softly. "Easy, boy."

Halfway down the path, Dylan saw the threat. At first, he thought it was another crossbow, but upon closer examination, he realized it was worse. It was a weapon he'd seen in action only once, but that once had been more than enough. His older brothers had brought it back from a safari in Sudan. Charlie had been fascinated by it. Like the crossbow, its velocity was deadly. But instead of arrows, it fired bolos: two steel balls attached to ends of a razor-like chain that wrapped around the throat and sliced through flesh and bone like butter. Back when they'd first acquired the weapon, Brady and Tom had set up a range along the beach, using pineapples and melons as targets. They'd offered Dylan a shot, but he'd declined. Charlie had jumped at the chance and turned out to be a crack shot with the exotic weapon. The party had ended when Morgana arrived and read off the two oldest boys for allowing Charlie to play with such a dangerous weapon. Much to the chagrin of Brady and Tom, the bolos had been permanently retired to the Armory after Morgana had complained about it to the old man at dinner.

Dylan gazed at the deadly weapon now, his heart hammering a slow driving beat inside his chest. It appeared to be aimed at the stone statue of Venus, which stood in the center of the fountain just behind Hakhan. As long as the dog stayed down, he would be safe. But if he stood at full height, he would be directly in the line of fire.

Unlike the crossbow that had been aimed at Beto back in the alcove, there was no infrared sensor to trigger this weapon. No countdown clock nor hunting knife to facilitate a timely rescue. Charlie's generosity had begun and ended on that first leg of the challenge. There would be no more free passes. If Dylan wanted to claim his second "item of value," he would have to do so all on his own.

Dylan's mind was racing now. He had inched his way closer to the entryway of the cubby while managing to keep the dog in a prone position. But Hakhan was getting antsy, as if it were a game in which the goal was to spring before Dylan could get to him.

"Easy," Dylan said as the dog's hindquarters began to twitch with anticipation. "That's it, nice and easy does it—"

The sound came suddenly—a high-pitched tone that sent a wave rippling along Hakhan's back, raising his fur in hackles and causing his ears to stand bolt upright. It was a mechanical sound, like gears spinning and clicking into place. Out of the corner of his eye, Dylan glimpsed the subtle movement of the weapon atop the hedge wall. In a single blink, like a slow-motion shutter click of a camera, a red dot appeared on the face of the stone statue behind Hakhan, and for an eerie second, time seemed to stand still.

Then time resumed, and it happened, seemingly all at once.

Hakhan sprang up to his feet, blocking the statue of Venus. Dylan bolted forward. Hakhan sprang up and lunged forward too, but the chain around his neck stopped him. To Dylan's horror, the chain wasn't tethered to the base of the fountain but instead ran around it and trailed from there through a series of metal rings staked into the ground along the perimeter of the cubby. At the final ring, the chain ran up the hedge wall straight to the base of the weapon positioned at the top.

Just as the chain reached its limit and went taut—preventing the dog from going any farther and keeping him directly in the line of fire—Dylan skidded to a halt the same way he would on a soccer field and called out: "Incoming!"

Hakhan dropped to his belly at once and put his paws over his snout—a split second before the bolos came whizzing at him with blinding speed. They flew overhead and wrapped around the neck of the statue behind him, and as the steel balls collided, the chain between them cleanly decapitated Venus.

Hakhan was up in a flash and racing around the fountain to retrieve the "ball." The blood was pounding so loudly at Dylan's temples that he could not hear the labored grunting as the dog attempted to nudge Venus's stone head across the grass to him.

When Dylan dropped to his knees and called him over, Hakhan left the immovable "ball" and came running, with his tail wagging and a desperate whine pushing through the muzzle. With his heart still pumping wave upon wave of blood to his throbbing temples, Dylan removed the muzzle and unhooked the end of the chain attached to Hakhan's collar. He ran his fingers through the dog's fur. Hakhan barked once and then began pelting Dylan's face with kisses. Dylan continued to stroke his fur while cooing soothingly to him, "Good boy. Very good boy."

When the throbbing at his temples subsided, Dylan took the short piece of rope out of his pocket and held it out to Hakhan, who sniffed it thoroughly.

"You got it?"

Hakhan sniffed the rope again, and his ears perked up.

"That's Beto. He takes you for runs when I'm away. You know Beto."

Hakhan barked. Dylan held the piece of rope before the dog's earnest eyes.

"You go find him," he said. "Go find Beto."

Hakhan took a step back, planted his paws firmly, and snorted.

"I'll come find you in a minute. You go find Beto and take him back to the house."

Hakhan took another step back, angling to go. But then he looked back at Dylan again.

"I'll be right behind you. I'll come find you soon. Now go find Beto. It's all right. Go find Beto."

Hakhan held his gaze a moment longer before turning and racing back into the heart of the maze.

The watch on Dylan's wrist beeped, and he looked at the digital countdown. He had less than ten minutes to find Lexie.

14

Music rose in the night once again—another track from the *Batman v Superman* score—this time coming from the roundabout at the center of the maze. A low, thrumming composition entitled *Day of the Dead*, which opened with the Man of Steel theme but would eventually bleed into the mournful march of the Dark Knight. Back when they were kids—Dylan, eleven, and Charlie, seven—Charlie had created a playlist of all the music True Son had compiled for his showdown with the President—each track in the same order it had played on that fateful night. When Dylan had asked him what he was listening to, Charlie had lifted his headphones from his ears, looked Dylan in the eye, and replied solemnly, "Our legacy."

At the time, Dylan had just smiled curiously at his younger brother's odd response. But in the years following, as he learned more about their great-grandfather and the night his corrupt presidency had come crashing down upon him like a house of razor-sharp cards, Dylan would never fail to receive a chill whenever he recalled that seemingly innocuous moment when Charlie had lifted his headphones and spoke those two words: *Our legacy.*

Walking between the tall rows of hedges now, toward the swelling music, Dylan wondered if perhaps all paths, no matter which you chose, eventually led to an inevitable destination. A fated finale. Preordained and mapped out long before you were born. Your inescapable legacy, waiting patiently to embrace you at the end of your journey through the maze of your life.

Could it be that simple? Could it be that no matter what path you chose, you were destined to end up in a place that had been chosen *for* you? And if so, was there any point in resisting? Would it just be easier to fall in line and accept your fate?

Our Legacy.

Those words echoed through his consciousness now like a whisper down a distant well as he followed the haunting melody drifting on the night wind . . . a sweeping, majestic melody, beckoning him toward a destiny he'd been holding at bay with one arm while inviting it into his embrace with the other.

He had turned his back on the family long ago.

All save for one.

Please say you'll come, Dylan, please.

Charlie had been the single thread that tethered him to home. He had never been able to say no to Charlie, and when Charlie had called earlier this evening, begging him to come to the party, Dylan's response had never been in question.

Dylan reached the roundabout just as the final chords of the Man of Steel theme descended into the melancholic yet paradoxically stimulating adagio of The Dark Knight. He made his way along the curved outer wall with caution and halted just before reaching the gap between the hedges which formed the entryway to the roundabout. His heart was pounding again, and the pulse at his temples was throbbing. He tried to swallow, but his throat was too dry. Unless Charlie had decided to go against his own rules of fair play and toss Dylan a red herring, Lexie was inside the roundabout. And if what had happened with Beto and Hakhan was any indicator, she was in real danger.

The roundabout was the largest enclosure in the maze. Roughly twelve meters in circumference, it was formed by two curved hedge walls. Inside, three round hedges, each standing as tall as the half-moon walls which encircled them, were evenly spaced at the center of the circle, with the middle hedge blocking the view of the opposing entryways from each other.

Dylan took out his phone and used the flashlight to examine the entryway. When he found nothing, he turned the beam toward the tops of the hedges. There were no weapons aimed at the inside like there had been back at the other two enclosures.

It can't be this easy. What are you up to, Charlie?

He turned off the flashlight and slid the phone back into his pocket; the light might be helpful inside the darkened roundabout, but he wanted both of his hands free, just in case. In the absence of his phone's flashlight, he waited for his eyes to adjust to the dark. Then, he took a shallow breath and entered the roundabout.

It was dark inside the mask, and a bit difficult to breathe, too. How someone could spend an entire night inside such a close-fitting head covering was well beyond Charlie's comprehension. But then, the someone in question hadn't actually spent the entire night in the mask, had he? Several lengthy breaks had punctuated True Son's face-to-face with the President. And it hadn't been a real face-to-face, anyway, had it? The showdown had taken place via satellite because

True Son hadn't the guts to engage in a real face-off with his enemy.

Charlie's eyes shimmered with disdain behind the dark glass eyes of the mask.

Despite the masterful planning and brilliant execution (and make no mistake, what had happened on that night nearly forty years ago *was* an execution, a cowardly, back-stabbing assassination of a great man whose only crime had been his ill-fated attempt to bring an ungrateful nation back to its past glory), despite the admirable cunning and guile, True Son was nothing more than a silvered-tongued socio-path with a flair for the dramatic. And worse, he lacked the courage of his convictions.

If he'd had any backbone at all, he would have entered the Oval Office that night not via satellite but in person. He would have stood toe to toe with the President and looked him dead in the eye while plunging not a metaphorical blade but a *real* one straight through his heart. And as the old man choked out his last breaths, True Son would have removed his mask and demanded, *Can you see me now?*

Charlie drew a shuddering breath inside the mask and nearly swooned. In his mind, he could see his great-grand-father felled by True Son's steely blade in the Oval Office, and his heart swelled at the thought of such a magnificent ending for such a great man. A tragic and brutal death, but nonetheless, a grand and fitting exit for a man who had loomed larger than life itself.

Of course, it hadn't ended like that. It had ended with the deceitful media painting True Son in loving brushstrokes as a martyr while recreating Charlie's great-grandfather, their president, as a madman, a monster, an aberration to be locked away and never heard from again.

The thought of his great-grandfather—a once tower-ing and formidable man of incalculable means and limit-less power—drooling on himself in an asylum used to bring

Charlie's blood to a full boil, heightening his desire for revenge against all who'd turned their backs on their leader. But as Charlie grew, he learned not only how to contain his emotions but to use the fire they generated as fuel for higher purposes. And once he had donned this helmet and mask and seen through the eyes of True Son, the fog had lifted. And with his new clear vision, Charlie understood that revenge served no purpose beyond the short-lived pleasure derived from its climax. A fleeting pleasure that all too soon bleeds into bitterness and regret, for once your enemy is dead and buried, you can no longer enjoy his suffering—and worse, you lose the opportunity to turn him to your way of thinking.

Charlie took a shallow breath as he concentrated on the tiny holographic screen above the right eye inside the mask—a marvel of technology, considering it had been constructed by a novice nearly four decades ago. It had taken Charlie a great deal of time to get it up and running again and link it to the network of cameras he'd positioned throughout the maze. But now as he watched Dylan's progress on the little holo-screen, he felt it had been well worth the effort.

Dylan had recovered his first two items of value without a scratch on either. Of course, Charlie had been waiting and watching, with his finger poised over the fail-safe switch, just in case Dylan's reflexes weren't fast enough. It had never been Charlie's intention to harm the prizes. Not that he cared for either the Mexican or the mutt—indeed he wouldn't have minded removing both from the equation. But he understood that harming either would turn Dylan on him for good, and that was the last thing he wanted.

Still, he needed to send a message. He needed Dylan to understand the fragility of things most loved. He needed Dylan to understand that, without protection, what could be broken would be broken, and only through the use of power could those most vulnerable be protected. He needed Dylan to understand that together, through the strength and power of their united family, they could form an impenetrable shield over all they held dear. Dylan needed to understand this before it was too late.

But first, Dylan needed to be roused from his slumber. One could hardly achieve greatness by sleepwalking through life and daydreaming of an idyllic existence in some faraway place. Dylan needed to learn this basic lesson, and Charlie was the only one who could teach him.

The dark eyes of the mask gleamed under the light of the moon as Charlie's head pivoted smoothly toward the north entrance of the roundabout. It was time. Charlie took a deep breath as he raised the crossbow and took aim.

Dylan had covered every inch of the roundabout, but there was no sign of Lexie—not even so much as a hint that she had ever been here or a clue as to where she might be. Nothing. With just under five minutes remaining on the digital wristwatch, the first tendrils of panic began to creep at the back of his mind.

This couldn't be it. There had to be some clue. She had to be someplace nearby. Charlie was scrupulous to a fault and never set anything into motion without a payoff. Lexie *had* to be nearby. Dylan just needed to concentrate and think of all that Charlie had said to him tonight. There had to be a clue, and it would be an obvious one because Charlie did not deal in the abstract.

Dylan took a breath and let it out slowly, concentrating on the rules of the challenge. There had always been three clues, and Charlie's had always been the most difficult to solve. Not due to their complexity—indeed they weren't complex at all. It was their *simplicity* that had never failed to throw Dylan off.

You think too much, Dylan. The most unsolvable mystery is the one whose solution is staring you in the face right from the start. Now, lay out the clues and see them for what they are.

In his mind, Dylan laid out the clues that Charlie had presented back in the Gold Room.

The bundle of cash he'd given to Beto. The rawhide bone with Hakhan's tooth marks. And the love letter.

While the first two clues had led directly to Beto and Hakhan, the third had led to this empty circle at the center of the maze.

But why?

Why indeed, Charlie's voice chimed inside Dylan's head. *But then I suspect you already know the answer to that one, eh, Dylan?*

Dylan didn't strain for it. He just let it come to him in all its simplicity. And this time, the voice in his head wasn't Charlie's.

It wasn't me, you know . . . the love note . . . the one you found in your locker that day . . . I didn't write it. But I wish I had. It was actually pretty good.

As those words cascaded down upon him, Dylan understood that the final clue had not been misleading. It had led to the same dead end that the love letter had. Lexie had never been a part of Charlie's challenge because it wasn't she who had written the love letter. And since the author of the note remained anonymous, there was only one other person with whom it had a connection, albeit a threadbare one: the person who had stolen it from Dylan's room and kept it all these years.

"Charlie," Dylan whispered, sensing that his younger brother was near.

He was about to turn and call out to Charlie when a distinctive clicking sound cut through the silence—he hadn't noticed it, but at some point, the music had cut off—and then something whistled by his ear at a downward angle.

The sound that followed was identical to the one he'd heard back in the alcove a split-second after he'd cut Beto free and pulled him out of the path of the speeding arrow. This shot had missed Dylan by mere inches, and the slender bolt now protruded from the seat of the wooden bench behind him.

The second shot followed fast. It whizzed by Dylan's right ear and lodged into the backrest of the bench with a resounding wood-splintering crack.

The third shot came in just as fast and took a little something with it.

Dylan gripped his right arm, where the arrow had torn through the sleeve of his shirt and grazed the skin beneath, drawing blood. The stinging sensation was enough to break his paralysis. He dived for cover just as the fourth shot came whizzing in. It missed him completely. So did the fifth.

But the sixth did not. It struck home with a sickening sound, like an iron fist striking a side of beef.

For a staggered second, Dylan wasn't sure that he had actually been struck by the arrow. He lay crouched down on the crisp blades of grass, wondering if he'd just bumped into something, the edge of the bench perhaps. Or possibly he'd been struck by something other than an arrow, another of Charlie's booby traps, perhaps. It stung like a whipping branch—numbness, followed by an odd tingle. But the real pain didn't come until he tried to get up. His knee gave out instantly, and he crashed to the ground as a searing pain shot up his leg.

He didn't cry out, but he grunted through tightly clenched teeth.

A deathly silence followed, in which Dylan tried to still his pounding heart so that he might hear the sound of any more incoming arrows.

The silence continued for a moment longer. And then something shifted in the darkness. A rustling sound in the hedges that could have been the wind, but Dylan knew better. And suddenly, he was scrambling backward, despite the agonizing pain, trying to get himself tucked into the shadows. He came to an abrupt stop when his back collided with the cold stone base of the statue at the east end of the roundabout. Tall and majestic, the statue of Eros loomed over Dylan like a guardian, with his wings fully spread and his bow at the ready.

But Dylan was well past the age of believing in fantasy. The threat was real, and no mythical hero was coming to save him.

He tucked his body into the shadow of the statue behind him, but his legs were still exposed to the shaft of moonlight that slanted down into the roundabout. He was able to pull his left leg up and into the shadow, but when he attempted to do the same with his right leg, another fiery bolt of pain shot up his thigh.

He looked down, and that's when he saw the arrow. It had penetrated the outside of his calf and broken through the skin on the other side. For a second, he was reminded of one of those gag arrows kids wore on their heads for Halloween, and he almost laughed as a crazy thought ran through his mind: *This can't be real.*

But it was real. The lower leg of his jeans was wet with blood, and the pain was throbbing so badly that a wave of nausea threatened to take him under. It was very real.

Taking shallow breaths, Dylan willed himself not to pass out. He took a deep breath and let it out slowly before making his next move. He tore the leg of his jeans where the arrow had penetrated. As he tied the strip of denim around his leg above the wound into a tight tourniquet, he thought of Lexie. She wasn't here in the roundabout, but that didn't mean she wasn't out there somewhere in the maze, and if there was even the slightest chance that she was a part of Charlie's plan, he had to figure out a way to get to her before . . .

The music rose from the speakers once again. This time, it was just The Dark Knight's theme—the same music that had been playing in the Oval Office when True Son had made his entrance on the TV screen above the mantle for the first time. The sound of that music playing here in the maze at Largo Morta sent a cold wave of tendrils racing over Dylan's body.

The moon shifted in the cold, dark sky above as if on cue, and its ray shone down on the north entryway, where the tall figure, dressed in black, now stood between the hedges, silently gazing down at Dylan through the glassy black eyes of the mask.

As the haunting music drifted down from the speakers, a lump rose to Dylan's throat and his eyes misted over. But he pushed back the emotion, along with the pain, and forced himself to look up into the soulless black eyes of the mask. Strength was the only thing Charlie respected, and right now, Dylan needed Charlie's respect more than ever. There was something dreadfully wrong, and he needed to take control before the situation reached the point of no return—that is, if it hadn't already.

Dylan steeled his nerves and said, "Where is she, Charlie?" It wasn't a demand, but it was firmly spoken so that there would be no ambiguity. When no response came, he pressed again in that same controlled tone. "Just tell me that she's safe—that she's not out there somewhere in danger. Just tell me that." It was impossible to completely still the tremors running through his body, but Dylan did his best to hold it together as he waited for Charlie's reply, which came after a moment.

"She's not a flower, Dylan. She doesn't need your protection. She can take care of herself. Trust me."

"Where is she, Charlie?"

Charlie took a breath, and for a moment it appeared he wasn't going to answer. Then, without exhaling, he said, "She's safe."

Dylan gazed up at the mask, but it wasn't the impenetrable glass eyes that made him doubt the veracity of his brother's claim; it was the voice modulator inside the breath screen which made Charlie's words come out in the eerily dispassionate tone of True Son.

"Swear it," Dylan said bluntly.

Another moment, and then the modulated voice issued forth once again: "I swear that she's safe."

But there was something different in the tone this time. Fear? Regret? Remorse? Dylan couldn't be sure. He took a breath, wincing at the pain, and said, "Take it off, Charlie."

The figure stood still, contemplating Dylan through the dark glass eyes, and Dylan waited a moment before repeating the request gently.

"Take it off."

For an eerie second, Dylan wasn't sure his words had gotten through, or, even if they had, that Charlie would comply. Had it been anyone other than Dylan making the same request, the mask would have most certainly remained on Charlie's head until he was ready to remove it.

Dylan waited, and after a measured moment, Charlie set down the crossbow and reached up with both hands to disengage the helmet and mask. It came off smoothly and in one piece, and when it fell to the grass with a soft, anticlimactic thud, Dylan breathed a silent sigh of relief as if the worst had passed.

But when Charlie ran his fingers through his sweaty hair and looked down at him, a sudden shiver raced through Dylan. It was as if Charlie had removed one mask only to reveal another beneath it. Dylan's mouth hung agape for a moment, and then he spoke.

"I know you didn't mean to do this. I know that things just got out of control. All of this . . . the party, this night, everything. This isn't you. I know that, and you know it, too."

Charlie smiled, a queer smile that made Dylan uneasy. "How do you know that?"

"Because I know you."

A brief flicker in Charlie's eyes, and then his strange smile deepened. "Do you, Dylan? Do you know me? Do you really know me?"

With his heart pounding fiercely, Dylan forced himself to speak in a calm tone. "I know you better than anyone. I may not understand what's going on with you right now, and that's my fault. I never should have left things the way they were after our argument at Cambridge. I should have come to you sooner. I should have been there with you after the election—"

"You mean *during* the election, don't you?"

"I couldn't go through that right then. There were a lot of things going on with me, and I just couldn't be around the family. I tried to tell you that at Cambridge, but you were upset—"

"I was upset, Dylan, because you turned your back on me," Charlie said evenly. "I came to bring you home so that you could spend the most important night of Father's life with the rest of the family. Even if you don't support Father's politics, you could have at least been there for the rest of us . . . for me . . . the person you claim to know better than anyone, the person you claim to love—"

"I do love you," Dylan said, his voice suddenly choked with emotion.

"You have an odd way of showing it."

Dylan forced the emotion back and said, "When have I ever turned my back on you. When have I ever not immediately come when you called?"

"I've just told you, silly," Charlie said with that strange smile. "Are you deaf?"

"One time, Charlie. One time I couldn't be there, and not because of you, never because of you. I couldn't be there because of him. I couldn't be there if he won—knowing what he is and what he would have done . . . the damage he's capable of, I couldn't be there for that. And if he lost, what would I be able to do? Everyone in the family knows how I feel; it's not like I could have consoled any of them."

"You could have consoled me."

"And you would have believed that?"

Charlie gazed at Dylan in stupefied wonder. "Why do you hate us?"

"I don't hate you."

"Yes. Yes, you do. You hate us. You hate our family so much."

"I don't hate our family. I disagree with them, Charlie. But I don't hate them."

"You hate Father!" Charlie snapped with sudden vehemence. "Can you deny it? Can you look me in the eye and deny it?"

Dylan looked him in the eye but didn't reply.

"Admit it, Dylan. You never loved Father."

Dylan's lips parted as he searched for an answer that wouldn't shatter his younger brother. He settled on the truth. "I wanted to love him."

"What does that even *mean?* You either love someone or you don't. You can't *want* to love a person that you hate. Do you hear how crazy that sounds?"

"Yeah," Dylan said, his voice scarcely breaking above a whisper. "Yeah, I do."

It was quiet for a moment, save for the undulating music. Then Dylan shifted, and another bolt of pain shot up his leg. He winced as he braced his back against the base of the statue. A moment passed, and then he looked up at his brother and said, "I'm leaving, Charlie. You can leave, too. You're almost seventeen. You could come with me. We could go see a judge, and I can petition for custody of you. Temporary guardianship, just till you're of age. I can get you out of here."

Charlie laughed in confusion. "Get me out of here? What are you *talking* about? This is our *home*, Dylan."

151

"No," Dylan said, "it's not. I don't know what it is, but it's not a home. It hasn't been a home since Mom died."

"*My* mother, you mean."

"She was my mom too."

"No, Dylan, *your* mother was a Swedish whore, who seduced Father and died a perfectly natural death. *My* mother was a hell-bound pythoness, who *bewitched* Father, as well as you, and paid for her many sins by drowning herself in a tub of her own blood. Because she wasn't brave enough to stay and protect her own son. Don't you dare try to paint her out to be a seraph just because she showed you a modicum of affection. Look at you! Who wouldn't love you? You're perfect."

Dylan shook his head even though the effort sent a dizzying wave coursing through him. "She loved you, too, Charlie. She loved you so much, you just don't know—"

"I know!" Charlie shouted. "Don't tell *me* what I don't know! *You're* the one who doesn't know! *You're* the one who's weak! *I'm* the stronger one now! *I* have the power now! *I'm* the stronger one!"

The blood was crashing at Dylan's temples again, but he managed to speak calmly. "You've always been the stronger one, Charlie." He wasn't sure if he should press it further, but the tentative look in Charlie's eyes gave him hope. "And Dad knows it. They all know it. That's why they work so hard to keep you under their control. They want you to believe that you could never make it without them. But the truth is, you can. The truth is, you're a lot stronger—and smarter—than I was at your age."

Dylan let that last statement sink in before going on, and Charlie made no attempt to cut him off this time.

"We can leave here tonight," Dylan said. "We can just get in my car and drive, doesn't matter where, anyplace far away from here, leave it all behind. All you have to do is say the word . . . "

Charlie wasn't looking at Dylan anymore. He was looking down at the mask of True Son, the tortured soul who'd finally had enough and taken a stand. Right or wrong, True Son had cast aside all doubt and shoved his entire stack into the pot that night. He had risked everything for his beliefs.

Charlie didn't know if he had the courage to take such a risk for his own beliefs—certainly not when he wasn't entirely sure just what his beliefs were. But he knew that winning wasn't really winning if you weren't there to scoop up the pot after revealing the best hand. The only question was, did he actually *have* the best hand? Was Dylan right? Was the family bluffing against Charlie's inside straight? Or were they holding a well-disguised full house, secretly smiling and patiently waiting to call the moment Charlie shoved? And make no mistake, that was precisely what Dylan was asking him to do right now. Throw caution to the wind and blindly shove all-in against the family.

Charlie's lips parted tentatively, but when he spoke, he did not look at Dylan; he just continued to gaze down at the mask of True Son.

"Do you know what it's like when the voices start inside your head, Dylan? Do you know what it's like when they all start speaking at once—Father, Grandmother, Great-grandfather—do you have any idea what that's like?" He shook his head, sadly. "You say 'leave' because it's so easy for you. You're used to leaving—you've been doing it your entire life. That's OK. I'm not blaming you. I know your weakness—it's the reason you're lying there bleeding and I'm still standing. But I know your strength too. I know that you don't hear those voices because you blocked them out a long time ago, and I'm happy for you. But what about me? Where can you take me that the voices can't follow? Where can you hide me from that?"

The emotion welled inside of Dylan again, but he pushed it back. Charlie needed his strength now. "I can get

153

you help. We can find someone to help you with that, someone to talk to."

Charlie laughed a humorless laugh as his eyes brimmed with tears. "What, a shrink? Someone to probe around my abnormal thoughts? Give me some pills, maybe? We've got cabinets full of pills right here. You think some doctor can make me normal like you? You don't think I've already *tried* to be normal like you?" He sniffed. "It doesn't work like that, Dylan. You can't remake me into another you."

"I don't want you to be me—"

"You just want me to be normal."

"You *are* normal. You've just been through a lot of shit and need someone who can help you sort it all out."

"You think I'm crazy?"

"No."

"You think I need to get away from the family because I'm crazy, and if I stay I'll only get crazier?"

"I think you're confused right now. I think there are things going on inside your head that you can't understand, but that doesn't make you crazy. I had the same problems when I was your age—"

"Did you, Dylan?" Charlie snapped. "Did you hear the voices inside your fucking head?"

"I heard the same crazy shit you did. And I tried to protect you from it."

"And just look at me now," Charlie said with an ironic smile. He tilted his head back to keep the tears from falling.

"It's not you, Charlie," Dylan said gently. "None of this is you. It's—"

"If you say it's Father or Grandmother or Great-grandfather," Charlie said with his head still tilted back to keep the tears from spilling, "I'll kill you, Dylan."

It came out just like that. No passion, no anger, nothing remotely resembling emotion of any kind. Just a simple statement of fact.

Silence followed, as if everything had suddenly been sucked into a black hole.

And then Charlie spoke again in that same dispassionate tone. "Tell me something, Dylan . . . and I'll know if you're lying, so don't . . . did you vote for Father?"

Dylan sat stunned and speechless, believing that this moment—right here in the maze, from which he had once rescued his younger brother—could be his last; believing that his life could actually end at the hands of the only person he would willingly die for without hesitation. With this realization, something shifted inside of him, and he knew that no matter what happened next, he would not lie; he would not sugarcoat the truth, nor dull its sharp edges. And, above all, he would not beg for his life.

Charlie was still looking up at the sky when he said calmly, "I'll ask you once more, Dylan: Did you vote for Father?"

Dylan's gaze was locked on his brother. But he remained silent.

Defiant. Obstinate.

Charlie snapped without warning and bolted forward. The heel of his shoe came down hard on the shaft of the arrow protruding from Dylan's calf, sending a bolt of searing pain up his leg. Dylan winced but did not cry out. And suddenly they were face to face, Charlie's mouth twisted into a vicious snarl.

"DID YOU VOTE FOR FATHER?"

Gritting his teeth and gazing directly into Charlie's wild eyes, Dylan grunted defiantly, "No."

He added nothing more, but Charlie could see the truth in his eyes speaking loudly and clearly: *I voted for* her, *and I'm glad she beat him.*

And that was all it took.

Quick as a whip, Charlie sprang backwards, snatched up his crossbow, aimed it at Dylan, and fired.

15

A wave of gasps rippled throughout the Gold Room. Looking up at one of the screens high above, Xander Grach chuckled nervously to his buddies, "I know it's not real . . . but, you gotta admit, it *looks* real . . . I mean, it *can't* be real." He shook his head with a lopsided, awestruck grin, knowing that what he was seeing couldn't possibly be real, even as a chilly shaft of doubt crept into his heart. And with another nervous chuckle, he shook his head again, this time in stunned admiration. "Man, Charlie is like a psychotic evil theater geek genius . . . he should be in Hollywood or something . . . this is some crazyass shit!"

The entire crowd watched in eerie fascination, believing that it had to be a put on—there was simply no way they had just witnessed Charlie Latner shoot his older brother with a real arrow. One of Charlie's classmates, a tall, skinny kid with a shock of bright red spiky hair, drew an awed breath and whispered to his buddy, "This is gonna get a *kajillian* hits on Rewind . . . *God, I wish I'd thought of it!*"

The only person in the Gold Room who wasn't

watching in appreciative awe was Phil Parma, Dylan's old soccer buddy who had gone to work for Dylan and Charlie's father straight out of college. After coloring up his chips at the blackjack table in the Atrium and cashing out, Phil had decided to call it a night. But on his way to the lobby, he'd heard the commotion coming from the Gold Room, and his curiosity had gotten the better of him.

Now as Phil Parma stood at the back of the hall, watching the eerie show play out on the big screens, he was grateful that he had taken this detour instead of heading straight to the lobby. Under other circumstances, Phil might have been wooed into believing that what he was witnessing was an impressive bit of cinematic art, designed and executed by a particularly talented teenager with a bright future in the film industry. The arrows protruding from Dylan's body, as well as the blood flowing from the wounds, could easily be the result of exceptional visual effects—kids were posting all sorts of pseudo-reality videos online these days. The incendiary dialogue could be the product of a wildly over-the-top imagination—teen angst-motivated violence scored mega hits on social media.

But the one thing that couldn't be faked was Dylan's reaction—the anguish on his face when Charlie had stepped on the arrow protruding from his calf; the look of resignation in his eyes just before Charlie had aimed the crossbow at him for the second time and pulled the trigger. Phil had known Dylan since they were teenagers and, without reservation, could say that he'd never met a more authentic individual in his entire life. The guile it would take to pull off such a harrowing performance was simply not in Dylan Latner's arsenal. There was no doubt in Phil Parma's mind that the disturbing scenario being played out on the suspended TV screens in the Gold Room was real.

Phil didn't waste time thinking about who to call. He reached into his pocket, pulled out his mobile phone, and dialed the only person who held sway over Charlie.

. . .

The arrow had pierced Dylan's chest, high and close to the left shoulder. At such close range, it had driven all the way through, pinning him to the base of the statue. At first, the pain had been exquisite, a fiery bolt exploding in his shoulder and radiating down the left arm. He clenched his teeth to keep from crying out in agony. Then his body was bathed in cold sweat, and a dreamy sort of numbness crept over him. His eyelids felt heavy, and he wanted to close them—just for a moment until he got his bearings back. But somehow he knew not to do that. Somehow he knew it was critical to keep his eyes open and not lose consciousness.

He looked up at Charlie through glassy eyes, thinking, *When did he get so tall? And why is he dressed like that?*

His eyes drifted down to the black mask on the grass, and then he remembered. *That's right. He's True Son.* And then he smiled curiously because that couldn't be right. True Son had died long before either of them was born. Charlie was just Charlie, and he'd gotten lost in the maze. And now that Dylan had found him, he needed to guide him out of the maze and back to the house. It all made sense now . . .

Dylan had started to drift again when a familiar sound brought him back. He looked up as Charlie took a second hit off his inhaler and thought, *That's it, breathe. You're safe now, Charlie . . .*

The haze threatened to draw him under again. And it likely would have had Charlie not bent to one knee and placed a hand on his shoulder—not the wounded shoulder, but the result was the same. A bolt of searing pain shot through Dylan and brought him back to full consciousness.

Charlie retracted his hand with an apologetic smile. "Look at you, Dylan," he said, gently, dreamily. "You're so fragile. I just want to take you into my arms and shield you from all the things that could harm you out there in the world . . . "

He reached out tentatively, but when Dylan flinched, he retracted his hand again and smiled a sad smile.

"You have no idea of the dread out there," he continued. "We've been blessed, Dylan—truly blessed—to have been spared all that. The degradation, the *commonness* of that existence. But we can change it. We can help those people out there—those who weren't born special like us. We can lift them up, give them a better life. Not like ours, of course, because they're not like us and could never be like us.

"But we can make things better for them. I believe that. Father believed it before they broke him. Grandmother still believes it. And I can make you believe it if you let me. If you let go of all these radical ideas of yours . . . "

Charlie took a short breath, and for a second Dylan thought he might need another pull from his inhaler. But Charlie didn't reach for the inhaler. He just continued to gaze into Dylan's eyes as he went on.

"You can't escape who you are or where you come from. You and I are the descendants of the greatest man to ever hold the highest office in this country—the Leader of the Free World—and oh, how he cherished and fought for that freedom. For *everyone*, Dylan, not just the brave patriots who supported him. For every single American. He tried so hard to make us great again, to keep us protected from those who threatened to shake the very foundation of our Constitution." His eyes suddenly grew wide. "And look what's happened! Caitlyn Price has cheated her way into the presidency! Where her grandmother failed, she has succeeded. This is what Great-grandfather was worried about—it's precisely what kept him up tweeting till all hours of the night! But it's not too late to turn back the clock. We can do that. We can turn the tide—we're strong enough to do that, you and I. We're the only ones who can fix this mess!

"Our great-grandfather was a man of remarkable vision, but, as great as he was—and he was truly, truly great, I know you know that, Dylan—he was also flawed. His genius was

159

unparalleled, but like many other geniuses before him, it eventually drove him to madness. He just couldn't contain the fire within. It burned too bright. And in the end, it consumed him. Father suffered the same fate. He couldn't contain the fire within, and he couldn't control it.

"But *I* can. I can control the fire and make it do as I command. And with you at my side, I can *contain* it. You've always been able to reach me and soothe the flame without snuffing it. You're my muse and my guardian, and you can keep me from burning too brightly and descending into the same madness that swallowed our father and great-grand-father. You can *save* me, Dylan. That's your purpose. You were born to save me . . . *from me.*

"It all makes such perfect sense once you open your eyes and see. And you have the eyes to truly see. You've been doing it your entire life. You've seen crisis after crisis and taken the necessary steps to avert each and every one. I would have killed somebody by now if it weren't for your gentle guiding force easing me back from the brink, we both know that.

"You're the water that cools my fever. You're the air that gives my flame its breath while simultaneously keeping it from raging out of control. You, Dylan. It's always been that way. Surely it hasn't escaped you—all those times you pulled me back from the abyss just when I was on the precipice of taking that fatal step."

In a series of flashes, Dylan could see the key moments of his life—Charlie's life—racing through his mind like snapshots on a film reel . . .

The dinner table, just before he'd thrown up. His stomach churning, his pulse racing as he watched Charlie gaze at the old man chewing and swallowing. And then his own gaze dropping to Charlie's small hand curling around the handle of the steak knife on the crisp, white tablecloth beside his untouched dinner plate. Dylan had known then what Charlie had intended to do with that knife. He hadn't wanted to believe it, but he had known it in his gut. And had he not thrown up right then and there, he was certain the quiet family dinner would have had a far more gruesome conclusion.

The bathtub. Charlotte's arm dangling over the side, the last few drops of blood dripping from the vertical openings in her wrist. Charlie's gaze fixed not on his dead mother but rather the blood-streaked razor—seeing a release that could only be provided by that sharp, shiny blade which had fallen from his mother's fingers to the cold tiled floor. Had he not been there to break down the door, Dylan knew that Charlie would have eventually found the passkey, entered the bathroom, and joined his mother in the tub.

The bullying at school, which the old man had brushed off. After Charlie had come home with the black eye, Dylan had made sure to fly home from Cambridge every Friday and spend the entire weekend with Charlie. And during the week, he'd never failed to contact Charlie every night for a calming chat. Dylan had done this because he'd seen the look in Charlie's eyes and feared that Charlie, once so obsessed with teen slasher flicks, might take the step from fantasy to reality and exact revenge upon his tormenters at school . . . a revenge where the killer would succeed in dispatching *all* his victims.

Now as he lay back against the stone statue of Eros with spread wings and bow and arrow held at the ready, Dylan knew that his brother was right. He had always been there to ease Charlie back from the edge of disaster. And Charlie had been aware of it the entire time, even back when Dylan had still been in the dark.

Dylan released a shuddering sigh as the revelation washed over him in a cold wave. Charlie had known all along that Dylan was protecting him from acting on his darkest impulses. Only now, in an ironic flip, it was Dylan who needed protection. Perhaps, deep down, Dylan had known this day would eventually come, that after deflecting

Charlie's rage for so long, it would have no other target to turn on but him.

As if reading his older brother's thoughts, Charlie said, "You don't want to turn on me, Dylan. Without you, there's nothing left for me."

Dylan took a breath, steeling himself against the pain. But he remained silent.

Charlie blinked with an awkward smile. "Don't make me beg you, Dylan."

Dylan held his brother's gaze like a skilled trainer dealing with an animal of dubious temperament and spoke as calmly as he could manage. "I'm leaving here, Charlie. And I want you to come with me. I want that more than you can know. But either way, I'm leaving."

Charlie's features froze for an endless series of seconds before the dam broke and the rage sprang forth. It came with the force of a tidal wave, surrounding his senses like a tunnel through which his focus was aimed solely at Dylan. And as Dylan expected, this proved to be his brother's undoing, for, like their great-grandfather, Charlie most often fell victim not to his adversary but rather his own hubris and unbridled temper.

Charlie did not hear the approach of the rapid footfalls as he stood up and loaded another bolt into the crossbow. Nor did he see the leaping blur on his periphery as he aimed the crossbow squarely at Dylan's chest. Indeed it wasn't until the powerful jaws and sharp teeth clamped down onto his forearm that Charlie's senses came back to him. And by then, it was too late.

Charlie flailed at Hakhan, who had sprung seemingly out of nowhere, but the huge dog only sank his teeth in deeper and shook harder in a fierce effort to disarm his master's assailant.

Dylan's eyes grew wide when he saw the Crossbow angle toward Hakhan. He gnashed his teeth against the pain as he pushed his body forward in a vain attempt to dislodge the arrow that pinned him to the base of the statue.

Unaware that the weapon was now pointed dangerously close to his underside, Hakhan growled as he continued to yank Charlie's arm. With equal determination, Charlie held on as he struggled to maneuver the dog into the hedge wall, where he could pin him with his free arm and get off a shot that would bring the conflict to a swift and decisive conclusion.

And then he would deal with his traitorous brother.

But the ending came even more swiftly and decisively than Charlie could have imagined when another interloper suddenly sprang from the entryway of the roundabout and leapt onto Hakhan's back. For a split-second, Charlie's eyes lit up with mad glee at the thought of Morgana's filthy feline coming to his rescue.

Then came the hiss, followed fast by the razor-like claws swiping across Charlie's cheek and the bridge of his nose, sending a warm spray of blood into his left eye. Charlie twisted, the crossbow shifted, and his finger jammed against the trigger. A millisecond of numbness followed. And then a blinding bolt of pain shot straight up his leg.

At once, Hakhan released Charlie's arm, Akasha leapt down from Hakhan's back, and Charlie collapsed against the hedge wall behind him, his foot pinned to the ground by the misfired arrow.

Akasha went straight to Dylan while Hakhan stood rigid and poised for defense, his fierce gaze locked on Charlie. But the fight was all out of Charlie now—at least the physical fight was.

As the brothers stared at one another in silence, a sound rose in the distance—a helicopter blade slicing through the dark sky—and Charlie's lips curled into an ugly grin.

"You think this makes you the winner, but you're wrong."

With effort, Dylan shook his head. He didn't want to be the winner. But he no longer possessed the strength to speak, and so he just held his brother in his gaze.

Charlie wasn't buying it. And he wasn't finished, either.

"You think you're going to walk off into the sunset and have a happy ending?" Charlie chuckled mirthlessly. "Not this time, Dylan. You don't get to be the hero this time."

Charlie coughed and grimaced and chuckled again. Dylan just continued to stare at him, trying to hold onto consciousness. But when the bright searchlight shined down on the roundabout at the center of the maze, Dylan closed his eyes and released a slow breath. Not in relief but in resignation. And as the searchlight pulled away and the helicopter came in for its landing on the stretch of lawn just east of the maze, the last of Dylan's resolve faded, and he drifted to the sound of Charlie's voice, scarcely audible, cutting in and out above the sound of the helicopter's whirring blade . . .

"You think you can have her without me? You think that's how it works? I *gave* her . . . *I* pull the strings! I *gave* her to you, and I can take her back . . . "

And then Charlie's voice faded completely, and there was nothing but the sound of the helicopter blade, spinning and spinning.

Of course, the night wasn't over yet—indeed, with the arrival of the family helicopter, it was only just beginning. But Dylan didn't care about that. He was exhausted and needed sleep. He'd had enough drama for one night and had no desire to fight Charlie for their grandmother's attention. When she made her dramatic entrance, Charlie could pull the strings and reel her in and have her all to himself.

As the last light of consciousness went out, Dylan slipped gently away, not realizing that Charlie's rant about "her" (*I gave her to you, Dylan, and I can take her back*) had nothing to do with their grandmother.

16

In the depths of his long slumber, Dylan didn't have a single dream that he could recall upon waking. At one point, he'd thought he was dreaming, but it turned out he was actually semiconscious and viewing an argument at his bedside between his father and grandmother. The old man was on a rant about "that fucking mutt" and "that evil fur-bitch," which Dylan understood to be Hakhan and Akasha.

"I might not be able to catch that sneaky little foo-foo fur-bitch—she's a cunning little whore and knows how to hide—but that fucking mutt is as stupid as they come, and I'm gonna kill him. I'm gonna go down to that kennel and personally shoot him myself!"

Grandmama Lona, whose tolerance for hyperbolic outbursts was legendary, simply sighed. "Calm yourself, dear, before you go into apoplectic shock. Your only concern right now should be the boys."

"That mutt nearly took Charlie's arm off!"

"Don't exaggerate, dear. Charlie's arm will be fine. The doctor said there's no permanent damage, thank God."

"That mangy mutt is dead. I swear I'm gonna shoot him dead myself."

"Oh, for the love of Pete, you don't even know how to load a gun, Jacob, and you certainly don't possess the fortitude to fire one, so be quiet."

The old man seemed stumped by that one, and Dylan's lips curled into a small smile as he looked at the two of them through the hazy slits of his eyes.

"Oh, look, Jacob," Grandmama Lona said sweetly, "he's smiling at us." She leaned in and stroked Dylan's hair, which made Dylan feel sleepy again, and so he drifted off to the gentle sound of her cooing, "There's Grandmama's handsome boy . . . "

She had called Dylan her "handsome boy" since as far back as he could remember. But she had never used this particular term of endearment for Charlie. Instead, with the same look of love in her eyes, she would call Charlie her "clever boy." And when referring to them both, she would say, "Don't they just make the perfect pair?"

"Looks like somebody's awake."

Dylan's gaze slowly moved around the room, which looked more like a small suite in a luxury hotel than a care unit in a hospital. The nurse looked up from the digital chart at the foot of the bed and smiled at him. Dylan's throat was too dry to speak, so he just nodded.

"Do you want some water?"

Dylan nodded again, and when the nurse held the cup with the straw to his lips, he drank without stopping.

"Take it easy," the nurse cautioned with a good-natured chuckle. "We don't want you to choke to death after all we did to bring you back."

Dylan finished drinking and looked at the nurse's ID badge, which read: DIEGO ROJAS, R.N. With his youthful appearance, lean build, and chiseled features, Diego looked more like a member of a boy band than a nurse.

Dylan asked, "Did I die?"

Diego laughed. "No. We're pretty good at what we do here, but we haven't perfected resurrecting the dead yet. But you did lose a lot of blood. The tourniquet around your leg probably saved your life—that was quick thinking; you definitely earned your first aid badge." Diego dropped a wink and grin, and Dylan smiled with a shade of embarrassment rising to his cheeks. "Hey, you're getting some color back. You were as pale as a ghost when they brought you in, hermano."

Dylan's smile faltered as the memory of the maze came back to him, and he said, "There was another guy in the maze with me—"

"Your brother," Diego said with a nod, "No worries. He's doing fine."

Dylan shook his head and with effort said, "No . . . my friend . . . Beto. Beto Larracuente."

Diego looked dubious. Dylan tried to lift himself higher on the pillow. Diego put out a hand to stop him and raised the incline of the bed with the remote. Then he gave Dylan some more water.

Dylan nodded gratefully and then looked Diego in the eye. "I just want to know that he's all right. He's my friend, and I just want to know that he's all right."

Diego looked around the room and then back at Dylan before speaking in a confidential tone. "He was admitted and released the next morning. No injuries. That's all I can tell you."

Dylan released a silent sigh and then asked, "Was there anyone else? A girl?"

"No. Just you three."

"You're sure? A redhead, about five-six—"

Diego's eyes lit with recognition, but he hesitated.

Dylan said, "You know who I am, right? I don't report to my family. This is just between you and me."

Diego hesitated and then said, "Yeah, she was here. She came to see you, but you were still out of it."

"How long was I—"

Dylan swallowed again, but before he could continue, Diego said, "A couple of days . . . Look, let me get Dr. Fuentes. She can tell you more than I can, OK?"

Dylan nodded, but it wasn't the doctor that concerned him. It was his grandmother. Because, in the end, hers was the only opinion that would matter.

She came to see him on the third day and shooed out the medical staff, who had just finished replacing the bandages on his calf and shoulder and were in the process of removing the IV from his arm.

"Is this really necessary," she asked in an airy tone. "I mean, can it wait?"

When the nurse attending to the IV told her yes, it was necessary, and no, it couldn't wait, Grandmama Lona sighed with a cursory eye roll and looked to the handsome young man in blue scrubs who'd dressed Dylan's shoulder wound, and queried, "Diego?"

Diego smiled apologetically. "It'll only take a moment, ma'am, and we'll be out of your way."

Grandmama Lona sighed again, but Dylan could tell that she was charmed by Diego and would offer no further protest.

When the nurses were gone, Grandmama Lona sat on the edge of the bed and placed a warm hand over Dylan's. With another sigh, she said, "Ah, that Diego, he's been such a blessing through all of this. I really don't know what we'd have done without him. I really don't . . . "

She looked around the room as if lost. But Dylan knew better. At seventy-five, his grandmother was in far better physical shape than the old man, who was twenty years her junior, and her critical faculties were as sharp as ever. Under normal circumstances, Dylan would have respectfully waited for his grandmother's theatrics to play out. But what had happened in the maze on New Year's Eve was anything but normal, even by *their* family's standards.

Dylan cleared his throat and said, "We need to talk about Charlie."

Grandmama Lona patted his hand with a sad yet sweet smile. "I know you're concerned about your brother, dear, but he's fine. There was no permanent damage to his foot, thank God."

"I'm not talking about his foot."

"It was a silly accident," she said with an airy sigh. "Children shouldn't play with dangerous toys—"

"They aren't toys," Dylan interjected. "They're weapons. And there's a room full of them at Charlie's disposal."

Grandmama Lona waved it off. "I've had that entire room cleared and spoken to your older brothers in no uncertain terms about acquiring any more of that claptrap." She gave Dylan a pointed nod. "It's as if none of those ridiculous things were ever there . . . so there's no need for any of us to worry about further incidents, dear."

Diversion by way of the veiled message was one of Grandmama Lona's favorite moves, but Dylan wasn't about to let the tactic work. Not this time.

"You can take away the evidence and pretend it never existed, but that's not going to solve the problem."

His grandmother laughed. "Oh, dear, you make it all sound positively Machiavellian. We are a family. We've got nothing to hide from one another."

"Or from anyone outside the family."

It was neither a question nor a statement, but Grandmama Lona got the implication, and her eyes narrowed ever so slightly as a clever smile curled at one corner of her mouth. "It's not polite to threaten Grandmama, dear."

Dylan's cheeks flushed. She brushed his hair back from his eyes with her fingertips and smiled her sweet, sad smile. For a moment, he wanted nothing more than to close his eyes and let her lull him into that false sense of security that worked so well on his father and brothers . . . just forget about everything that had happened and go his separate way after the spell had worn off and he could see clearly once again.

But he didn't close his eyes, because he knew that his grandmother's charm wouldn't work on him. Not this time. His eyes were finally wide open, and no amount of soothing smooth talk could get him to unsee what he'd seen. Something was wrong with Charlie, and someone had to stand up to the status quo the family cleaved to like a shield.

When she failed to penetrate the hard surface of Dylan's gaze, Grandmama Lona released a silent sigh and looked around the room again. Only this time, she didn't look lost. She waited a measured moment and then spoke in a tone that bordered nostalgia.

"I'd had such plans for your father—the governor's mansion was just a stepping stone to the White House. But as it turned out, he had too much of his grandfather's fire in him—my father, your great-grandfather, the President." Her eyes shimmered briefly and then dimmed. "But while your great-grandfather had a flourish with his fire—he was quite the showman, as you're doubtless aware—your father was all fire and no flourish. And in the end, the flames consumed him."

She paused and offered a curious smile, which made Dylan feel both warm and chilly at once.

"For a time I'd thought you might be the one. You have the stature, the natural appeal, and certainly the looks. But you lack the killer instinct, dear. Oh, you're competitive on the field, and you're certainly a winner—indeed a champion. But you're incapable of cannibalizing your own—your heart is too pure and gentle for that. You're not even capable of reining them in when they get out of sorts . . . "

Dylan's nostrils flared white as his cheeks burned crimson. Grandmama Lona patted his hand and offered a consoling smile.

"Charlie is a spirited colt, and he threw you because you haven't the heart to choke the bridle and dig in the spurs. It's not your fault, dear. Your virtue lies in your kindness and capacity to love beyond reason. But that virtue is also a shortcoming. It's your Achilles heel. Achilles was strong and handsome too, but in the end, he was defeated by love. The world is cruel and doesn't reward those who nobly sacrifice for love. Quite the contrary, it venerates those who are strong and cunning enough to recognize that love is neither worthy nor appreciative of sacrifice in its name. Indeed love is not a virtue to which one aspires but rather an obstacle to be conquered."

Dylan's eyes suddenly felt warm and wet, but he contained the emotion rising within. He held his gaze on his grandmother as he asked the question to which he most feared the answer. "Do you love me?"

Grandmama Lona looked genuinely surprised. "Of course, I love you. You're my grandson."

He wanted desperately to accept her answer at face value, but something inside made him push it one step further. "But you wouldn't sacrifice for me."

The statement hung there between them for a long moment, in which Dylan tried to make himself believe that he would receive the same response that any grandson would from his grandmother under the same circumstance. But he was not any grandson. He was Ilona Kingley's grandson. And as her chin rose, his heart sank.

"Your grandfather didn't grasp the concept either when your great-grandfather threw him under the bus," she said with a sad smile. "Not at first, anyway. But at the end, I truly believe he did." She sighed. "Had I known he was going to die so young, I would have visited him more often. But prisons are so depressing, and I didn't want to expose your father and uncle and aunt to that environment. It's a mother's job to protect her children, after all. And it's not like your grandfather didn't know what he was getting into. He was a good man, but not a blameless one."

As Dylan gazed at her with scarcely concealed wonder, he was reminded of something Charlie had once said when they were younger.

Sometimes when I'm in her presence—Grandmother, you know?—I can't breathe. It's like she draws all the oxygen in the room into her lungs, and it's like I'm floating in space, and she's the moon, and I'm held in her orbit. Have you ever felt that, Dylan?

At the time, Dylan had nodded in response to his younger brother's astute statement, but only now did he fully realize just how astute that statement had been.

As if reading his thoughts, Grandmama Lona smiled and said, "It was a long time ago, dear. When you've lived a bit more life, you'll understand that it's better to bury the past and move on."

She shook her head and sighed, and Dylan waited, knowing that she wasn't finished.

"Your father can be stubborn—much like my own father was. I gave your father my blessing when he decided to run for the presidency, fully knowing that he would never make it. Not that he couldn't have cut that little Crichton harlot off at the knees—*with* the proper advice, that is, which, of course, he would never accept. But I let him bat the mouse around and gave him my blessing as well as my money. His anger at his defeat will only fire up your great-grandfather's core base, of which there are many who've passed along the torch to an even angrier and younger generation, bless them. But my real hope has been invested in Charlie, who, unlike your father, is both malleable and stable."

Dylan gestured to his wounded shoulder. "You think

this is *stable?*" He waited for a response, and when none came, he went on. "Charlie isn't well. I don't think he's been well for some time. He needs help—not from you or dad or anyone else in the family. He needs professional help. He needs therapy." He paused to let it sink in—though, by his grandmother's expression, it was difficult to tell if any of it had. Then, without waiting, he added, "Charlie isn't stable, Grandma. He's dangerous. And if he doesn't get the help he needs, eventually, he's going to do something you can't cover up."

The old woman eyed her grandson as if sizing up an opponent across the boardroom table. She was impressed with his acumen—she had indeed taken the necessary precautions upon her arrival at Largo Morta on New Year's Eve. All of the mobile devices of the guests at the party had been confiscated, and their video contents had been erased, along with the master file in the security system. Bryanna Manners, head of PR at Tower K, had addressed the Gold Room guests and reminded them that their parents and grandparents were valued members of the Kingley inner circle, where discretion was held in the highest esteem. Of course, there was bound to be a few leaks, but without corroborating evidence, rumors were just rumors, and with the proper spin here and there, in time, all rumors faded.

Dylan could see the wheels spinning in his grandmother's head. She was easily the most confident individual he'd ever known. And she never bluffed. When she shoved, you could rest assured that she was holding a solid hand.

Only this time, things were a little different. This time, Dylan was holding a solid hand as well. And Grandmama Lona not only knew it; she was waiting for him to play it.

They sat contemplating one another for a long moment, Dylan weighing the strength of his hand against hers. Of one thing, he was certain: the spin was already out there—*New Year's Eve Party Game At Largo Morta Gets Out Of Hand; Two Sustain Minor Injuries.* Handpicked, carefully coached eyewitnesses, corroborating testimony from highly respected attending physicians, and a heartfelt statement by Grandmama Lona herself, assuring one and all that both of her grandsons were recovering nicely from their injuries and wished to thank all who sent kind wishes. Just a simple case of boys being boys. End of story.

But it wasn't a simple case of boys being boys, and it wasn't the end of the story. Despite all the manufactured testimony, Grandmama Lona's rewrite of history could be shot down by the dissenting statement of one witness: Dylan himself. It may not come to charges being filed, but it would certainly create an irreparable fracture in the family and sow doubt in the public consciousness for years to come.

But the destruction of the family was not what Dylan was after—he was far too noble for such an ignominious pursuit. Grandmama Lona could see it in his eyes, which had always been naked and pure. The ghost of a smile touched her lips at the sight of defeat in those naked eyes.

"Don't be a hater, dear," she said with a pleasant smile. "It's very unbecoming when focused on one of your own. Family trumps all else. Never turn on the family; it won't end well for anyone."

Dylan accepted his defeat—he wasn't capable of the tactics his family casually employed without compunction—but he held his gaze and gave one last attempt at appealing to his grandmother's better angels. "He could have killed me. You know that, right?"

"But you're alive!" she countered with a bright smile. "And now we can put all this nonsense behind us."

Dylan looked down at the white sheet folded over the coverlet, shaking his head. "I want him to be normal."

Grandmama Lona sighed. "Normal isn't normal, dear."

Dylan was still shaking his head. "He's just a kid. He can change. He doesn't have to be like this. He can get away from here. He can change if you let him go."

Grandmama Lona was silent, and for a moment, Dylan

thought he had reached a part of her that no one had seen or touched in many years, if ever. But when she finally spoke, he knew that he had only scratched the surface.

"And where would he go? We're his family. You're his family. You can't run away from family, dear; it has a way of catching up. If you truly care for your brother, stay here with him. He's always been lost without you, like a moon without a sun. Be his guardian. Guide him toward the light."

A tear fell from Dylan's eye and hit the fold of the crisp, white sheet, where it sat perfectly formed atop the starched surface. "I can't . . . I can't be complicit anymore."

Grandmama Lona chuckled softly, but the humor failed to reach her eyes. "Oh, my sweet, handsome boy," she said, with a forlorn smile, "if only it were that simple. But we are who we are—and have no delusions: we were born complicit."

She took his hand and pressed it to her lips, and for a while they sat in silence, neither of them able to look at the other. Then she set his hand gently on the coverlet and, without another word, got up and left.

Alone in the room that looked more like a posh hotel suite than a hospital care unit, Dylan tried to breathe but found it impossible.

This came as no surprise, of course.

Grandmama Lona had taken all of the oxygen with her.

17

Dylan left the hospital the day before his scheduled release and took a cab back to Largo Morta. Morgana had arranged a family dinner to celebrate his and Charlie's homecoming, though Charlie had been released a few days earlier and was already home. Dylan didn't relish the idea of blowing off Morgana's party—she had always been kind and often backed him up when he went toe to toe with the old man, especially when it concerned Charlie's welfare. But he couldn't bring himself to participate in another family gathering. Not after what had happened on New Year's Eve, and certainly not after the subsequent bedside chat with his grandmother at the hospital. He had to get away now, with or without Charlie, because if he stayed, he would eventually fall right back into his role of silent complicity, and he couldn't allow that.

Grandmama Lona had taken away his bloody clothes in a plastic bag and sent a fresh change of clothing to the hospital: a pair of single-pleat charcoal trousers by Ambrosi

Napoli, Démesure leather oxfords by Berluti, cashmere socks by Pantherella, silk boxers by Tom Ford, and a tasteful olive drab merino/linen crewneck sweater by her own label, IK{4}Him. An appropriate ensemble for the party but also a tangible measurement of her love. Over three thousand dollars worth, packaged in sleek boxes with avant-garde logos and designer signatures that reminded Dylan of the countless occasions his grandmother had taken him clothing shopping, from early childhood all the way through his senior year of high school. At times, Dylan had felt like he was little more than her life-size dress-up doll. But he never fussed like Charlie or complained like his older brothers. He just came from the dressing room in each of her selections, stood on the plushly carpeted platform before the triptych mirrors and dutifully turned so that she could view him from different angles while commenting to her personal shopper, "He has such a magnificent frame, doesn't he, Ambrose? The clothes absolutely adore him!" And occasionally, she would add with a chuckle, "My God, if he weren't my grandson . . . "

As the cab pulled up to the main entrance of Largo Morta, Dylan felt the sudden urge to swap out the new clothes for his own. But his bags were in the trunk of his car, which was parked in the private port on the residence side of the property. And he had no intention of going any deeper into the residence than necessary. The only stop he needed to make was on the ground floor, just off the glass corridor that connected the hotel to the residence. From there, he would head straight to his car and drive away without looking back.

Dylan crossed the hotel lobby unnoticed. Bypassing the private elevators in the glass corridor, he headed straight for the service elevator in the east wing—the slimmer the chance of running into anyone in the family, the better.

He didn't see any familiar faces until he reached the east

corridor, which was abustle with employees from Tower K in New York. The old man often conducted business out of his offices down here in Largo Morta, but rarely with such a workforce in tow. A few people smiled and offered brief salutations like "Hey, you're back!" and "How're you feeling?" as they passed by. But most were moving at such a brisk pace, they scarcely had the time to offer more than a cursory glance with a nod. Dylan was just grateful that no one stopped to chat.

He took the service elevator to the basement level and moved at a swift gait down the long central corridor. There was a dull pain in his calf, which was tightly wrapped under the right leg of his trousers, but he didn't let it slow him down. When he reached the adjoining hall halfway down the corridor, he took a short breath and turned left, hoping that his instinct was correct and relieved that it was.

The indoor kennels were only occupied during storms or when one of the dogs was either ill or delivering pups. The weather outside was beautiful, and the dog inside the first kennel was neither ill nor in delivery. He lay on the concrete floor with his chin resting on his paws. Dylan's heart took a tumble at the sight of the dog's sad eyes, but the emotion was immediately countered by anger at the sight of the muzzle. He gazed through the wide observation window for a moment before opening the door and stepping inside.

Hakhan's ears perked at once, and he attempted to bark, but all that came out was a low whine. He stood and wagged his bushy tail when Dylan approached, and when Dylan put his fingers through the chain link fencing, Hakhan tried to kiss them through the muzzle.

"Take it easy, boy," Dylan said softly. "I'm gonna get you out of here."

That's when a voice from behind him spoke up. "He can't go out."

Dylan turned to see a uniformed man that he didn't

recognize. He was tall and skinny and looked well past the age of retirement, especially for a security guard. The nameplate pinned to the breast pocket of his uniform read: F. DOBBS. He was armed only with a canister of mace on his belt, but he had the cagey look of one who might actually use it if push came to shove.

Dylan said, "What's your name?"

The old guy said, "Fred Dobbs."

"Fred, do you have the key to this lock?"

"Yeah," Fred said. "But he can't go out."

Dylan nodded like it was all good and said, "Fred, I need you to open the lock."

Fred nodded. "I can do that, but he still can't go out. He's a biter."

Dylan tried another tack. "Do you have a dog, Fred?"

"Two. Never bit no one, neither of 'em."

Dylan nodded and gestured with an open hand at the cage. "This is my dog, and I'm going to take him with me. He doesn't belong here."

"Well," Fred said, "he should've thought about that before he bit someone."

"I understand," Dylan said, holding his gaze on the old guy. "But I need you to get the key and open this lock right now."

Fred appeared to consider the request. Dylan remained calm while internally preparing himself for conflict. Even with his left arm in the sling against his chest, he was fairly certain he could take the old guy down before he could get to the canister of mace on his belt. But still, there was the possibility that Fred might be quicker than he looked, and Dylan wasn't itching to find out the hard way.

The tension, if it could be called that, broke when Fred turned away and retrieved the key from the hook behind the door. He unlocked the cage and stepped back without a word. Dylan opened the door, and Hakhan came out, snorting with excitement, his tail wagging eagerly. As Dylan unbuckled the muzzle's strap, Fred said, "You probably shouldn't do that. He's a biter."

"He's not gonna bite me, are you, buddy," Dylan said, stroking Hakhan's fur.

As the dog pelted Dylan with kisses, the old man made a noncommittal clicking sound with his tongue against his teeth. "I guess not," he said. He made the clicking sound again, more decisively this time, and sighed, "Well, just don't go blabbing it was me that let him out." Then he turned and left the room.

They were upstairs in no time, Hakhan eager to get out and race about the grounds but keeping pace at Dylan's side and not dashing ahead as he usually would. Dylan had planned to go straight through the lobby, where it would be difficult for security to prevent him from leaving without causing a scene in front of the hotel guests—Grandmama Lona had zero tolerance for public disturbances at Largo Morta, especially ones that involved members of the family. But at the last minute, he decided to take a shortcut.

At this time of day, most of the activity was centered in the north-east rooms of the ground floor residence while the large south-facing rooms, used primarily for evening gatherings, would be empty. A detour through the Red Lounge would take them to the back patio, and from there, a quick jot across the south lawn would take them to the private carport.

They passed the open doors of the Atrium, where sunlight pierced the vaulted glass ceiling high above and spilled along the polished ballroom floor in hazy streaks. The casino accoutrements had all been removed, leaving no trace of the New Year's Eve festivities. Indeed, it was as if the winning run he and Lexie had shared at the craps table on that night had been a dream or an illusion.

The Gold Room was vacant and silent too.

It wasn't until they reached the open doors of the Red Lounge that they encountered someone. And it was the last person Dylan expected to see.

She came around the corner at the end of the hall and stopped short. The look in her eyes was unmistakable; she hadn't expected to run into Dylan.

But there was something else in her eyes. A mixture of regret and guilt.

And then it was gone, and she was smiling. Not the smile she had given him on New Year's Eve. This new smile was cordial, formal, perfectly congruent with her sharp business attire: a long sleeve navy blue pencil dress that accentuated her figure and revealed just enough leg to pique interest. For a moment, Dylan was reminded of a younger version of his grandmother. And then the girl approached, and as she got closer, her smile appeared more natural. More like it had the night they'd made love in his room upstairs.

"You're back," Lexie said. "I didn't think you were coming home until tomorrow."

"I left early," Dylan said, looking into her eyes, searching for something he suspected he would not find.

"Well, all right," she said with a smile that should have put him at ease but for some reason didn't. She stepped forward and hugged him. He hugged her back with his good arm and scarcely felt the twinge of pain in his left shoulder. "I'm sorry," she said with a glance at his arm in the sling. "I didn't mean to crush you there. I didn't hurt you, did I?"

Dylan shook his head. He couldn't take his eyes off her. Even as she bent to greet Hakhan and accepted his tentative kisses with a warm laugh, Dylan couldn't take his eyes off her. And he couldn't shake the feeling that something had changed between them.

"So, do you work here?" he asked.

"Sort of," she said, still petting Hakhan. "Well, not here exactly—not for your father, anyway. I work for your grandmother. It's sort of an internship . . . at least when I'm not in school."

In his mind, Dylan could hear the voices from the maze that night—his and Charlie's . . .

Where is she, Charlie?

She's not a flower, Dylan. She doesn't need your protection. She can take care of herself. Trust me.

And farther back, buried in the depths of his memory . . .

You think you can have her without me? You think that's how it works?

Charlie had said this to Dylan right when the sound of the helicopter coming in for its landing on the east lawn was at its loudest. At the time, Dylan had thought Charlie was speaking of their grandmother. But looking into Lexie's eyes now, he understood that his brother hadn't been speaking of their grandmother at all.

I pull the strings! I gave her to you, and I can take her back . . .

Dylan flashed back on the events of New Year's Eve . . .

His chance sighting of the beautiful and familiar-looking auburn-haired girl in the Red Lounge when he'd stopped to ask his old soccer buddy, Xander Grach, if he'd seen Charlie.

I saw him heading upstairs, Xander had said. *He was talking with some hot girl, and then she whispered something in his ear . . .*

Their subsequent meeting in the glass corridor between the hotel and the residence.

I know you, don't I?

For about five seconds. I was a freshman when you were a senior.

Charlie's timely appearance from the elevator.

Lexie, this is my older brother Dylan. Dylan, this is Lexie . . . She's majoring in business management, just like you, Dylan.

So, who's going to give me the tour of this place?

It's New Year's Eve. You have to celebrate a little. And Lexie needs a tour guide. This is her first visit, and she'll get lost wandering around alone.

But it hadn't been her first visit. Looking into her eyes now, Dylan knew this. What he didn't know was how much of what happened later was just part of the act.

I want to see this bad boy you think you are.

I never said I was—

(You smell like sex, Dylan.)

No, but you think *it—*

(Next time you fuck one of my friends, have the decency to wash up after.)

Something shifted in Dylan's eyes—a scarcely discernible flicker, but Lexie saw it, and she understood that there was no point in lying. She looked at his arm in the sling against his chest and said, "I didn't know about the surprise . . . at least not the full extent of it. If I had, I would have called it off." She looked into his eyes again. "And if it makes any difference, I would have spent the night with you anyway. I wasn't lying about any of the things that I said."

Dylan pushed a strained smile. "Just the part about Charlie putting you up to it." He didn't intend it as a barb, but it took a little flesh with it when he pulled it out. "Just that part, right?"

"Just that part," she replied without looking away.

Dylan chewed at the corner of his mouth. "And the part about never being here before—"

"I didn't say that. Charlie did."

Dylan nodded. "And the part about working for my grandmother. Did she know about this too?"

Lexie shook her head. "No."

Dylan laughed suddenly, but it came out hollow, and there was no humor in his eyes. "I can't tell if you're in character or if this is the real you—you're that good at it." He gazed at her, searching her lovely eyes. "But I don't really know you, do I? You were just some girl watching me in the hallways at school, right?" He laughed again, that same clipped humorless laugh. "I don't even know if that part's true. You're an actress, right? *Molly's Game*, the back room poker madam." He shook his head without taking his eyes off her. "I'll give Charlie that much. He cast you well."

The sting of that one reflected in Lexie's eyes, but Dylan wasn't buying it anymore. They stood there for a long moment, neither willing or able to look away from the other. Hakhan's eyes shifted between them sadly, and then he nudged his head under Dylan's hand.

The silence broke when a voice spoke from nearby, "You two again, eh?"

Phil Parma approached from the opposite end of the hall with a glossy black folder in one hand and a curious smile on his face. Phil had visited Dylan at the hospital, but they hadn't spoken. Dylan had still been drifting in and out of consciousness, but he'd heard part of a conversation between Phil and Grandmama Lona as they stood at his bedside. Grandmama Lona had thanked Phil for his timely intervention on New Year's Eve and told him that she would not forget his loyalty and discretion. Phil had said that he was just happy Dylan was all right. And as an afterthought, he'd added, "And Charlie, too, of course." And then Dylan had drifted back to sleep.

"Am I interrupting something?" Phil asked with a preceptive glint in his eye.

Dylan shook his head. "No. How's it going, man?"

"How's it going with *you*?" Phil asked, giving Dylan a fist bump. "You don't look much worse for the wear," he added, with a glance at Dylan's arm in the sling.

Dylan shrugged his good shoulder. "I'm OK."

Phil gave Lexie a nod and a friendly wink. "Looking very retro Ilona Kingley this morning, Ms. Chalmers."

Lexie smiled. Phil was one of the few guys at Tower

K who had welcomed her without any strings of objectification attached. From day one, he had treated her like an equal, and his sly grins and teasing quips had never made her feel uncomfortable. Indeed he was like the older brother she never had.

"Nice dogs," Phil said with a casual glance at Dylan's shoes. "Better not let Scrooge McDouche and Sparky see them, lest they think you've stolen away Grandmama's favor."

Dylan smiled and shook his head. Scrooge McDouche and Sparky were Dylan's older brothers, Brady and Tom. And Phil was right; if they saw the Berluti shoes Grandmama Lona had bought for Dylan, they would likely go into panic mode, fearing she had written them out of the will.

Phil ruffled Hakhan's fur and said, "This guy come to bust you out of jail, Chomper?" Hakhan wagged his tail. Phil nodded. "Good timing. Get out while the old man's distracted."

Dylan's eyes narrowed with curiosity.

Phil raised a brow. "Ah, that's right, you've been laid up in the hospital for the past week. Well, thanks to your older brothers, Little Charlie's New Year's Eve Massacre has dropped to the bottom of your old man's bitch list."

"What happened?" Dylan asked.

"Not much," Phil said in his usual offhand manner. "Just the near collapse of a multibillion-dollar deal we've been working on for the past sixteen months. You know about the St. Claire Media merger, right?"

Dylan knew. The old man and Brady had gotten into a heated debate over it at Christmas dinner. It would have escalated to a full-blown fight if Morgana hadn't stepped in and told them no more business talk on the holiday. Grandmama Lona had backed up Morgana, and the old man and Brady had spent the rest of the family dinner fuming silently across the table from one another.

"Yeah," Phil said. "Well, your old man told Brady to

give everything we have on the merger to Scanlon—which was smart because Scanlon's got the eye of an eagle and the scruples of a buzzard, and his loyalty to your grandmother is unbreakable. So, of course, when your old man delegates, McDouche re-delegates and passes it off to Sparky, who then *emails* the files to Scanlon—which by itself is bad enough, but you know your brothers . . . "

Dylan nodded. He *did* know his brothers, but he asked anyway, "What happened?"

"Sparky accidentally CCed half the contacts on his phone, and so your old man's been in there all morning cutting checks and collecting NDAs."

"Is it serious?"

Phil shrugged. "Only a couple dozen violations that could keep your old man tied up in FCC hearings for the next six years." He clapped a hand on Dylan's good shoulder. "I gotta get back in there. He likes an audience, especially when he's reaming out your brothers." With a wink and grin, he added, "Drop me a postcard from wherever you're headed. I might need an escape hatch."

Dylan nodded, with a faint smile, knowing that Phil was only half joking.

Phil ruffled Hakhan's fur again and looked the dog straight in the eyes. "You take care of him, Chomper. Keep an eye out for any more stray arrows from paleface papooses on the warpath."

Dylan took no offense at the joke, but Lexie's cheeks flared red, and she glared at Dylan's old soccer buddy.

Phil, who didn't miss much, raised a casual brow and asked, "Too soon?" He gave Dylan's shoulder a squeeze. "Take care, man."

And then Dylan and Lexie were alone in the corridor again. Her cheeks were still burning and her eyes were still icy, but Dylan thought it had little if anything to do with Phil's quip about "paleface papooses."

He studied her for a moment.

Then he reached into his pocket and took out his phone.

The slight flare of her nostrils and cool sheen of her eyes told him all he needed to know without even having to scroll through his mail. But he did it anyway, and when he came to an email CCed to him from his brother Tom, he stopped and looked up at Lexie.

When she raised her chin, he smiled sadly because it reminded him of Charlie: the regal tilt of the head; the eyes staring down the bridge of the nose, defiant, stubborn. With Charlie, Dylan had always been able to break through that façade, usually with little more than a smile or a shoulder bump as they sat side by side.

But with Lexie, he could see no crack, not even the slightest chink. She was steely like his grandmother; once she'd iced over, no amount of smiling could melt her defenses.

But also like his grandmother, Lexie was practical and understood how the game was played.

Dylan eyed her thoughtfully as he calculated his next move. He had lost to his grandmother when they'd last spoken a few days ago in his hospital room. But that was only because his grandmother knew he would never play the cards in his hand. Not if it meant risking the possibility of sending Charlie to an institution—or worse, prison—for what had happened in the maze on New Year's Eve. He wanted Charlie to get the help he needed, but not at the cost of destroying his future. The stigma of being labeled the rich kid who'd shot and nearly killed his own brother with a crossbow would haunt Charlie forever, and no matter how he felt about Charlie right now, Dylan couldn't bring himself to destroy his younger brother's chance at a normal life.

But Phil Parma had just unwittingly dealt Dylan a new hand—one that Dylan could play against the family *without* harming Charlie. Indeed this new hand would ensure that Charlie got a fighting chance at a normal life.

He considered approaching his grandmother directly, but as he gazed into Lexie's eyes, he knew that wouldn't be necessary. He could make the deal right here and now with his grandmother's heir apparent.

He took a confident breath and said, "Here's what you're going to do—and this is not up for debate or discussion. You tell her that the price of my silence is based on the following conditions: First, Charlie is going to see a therapist. A real therapist—one who specializes in teenagers, not one of her gurus who tells you what you want to hear and fills out the prescriptions on command. And I expect to see the same updates she gets under the table from the therapist on a monthly basis. If she misses a single update, or if Charlie's therapy should suddenly stop, I release this email to her old friends at NCMSB—and the New York Times, The Washington Post, and a few other media outlets that she hasn't got in her corner."

He paused to make sure that Lexie had it all down, and when she nodded, he went on.

"Second condition: There's a kid who works here—Beto Larracuente." On Lexie's look of confusion, Dylan made it clear just who Beto was: "The kid who parks your cars for shit wages and cheap tips—the kid that Charlie used as a pawn in his little Hide-and-Freak game."

"He's not a freak," she said defensively.

"He's my brother, not yours. When he shoots you with a couple of arrows and threatens to kill you, then you can decide what he is."

It felt like a slap, but Lexie held her tongue and waited for the rest.

"Beto got used that night for something that he had nothing to do with, and the family is going to compensate him for his troubles by setting up a college fund. He's on a partial scholarship at the University of Florida, and it's about to become a full one. Don't set it up directly—no one from the family gets to be the hero on this one. Do it through a foundation—a legitimate one. He's an economics major with a three-point-eight GPA, so it should be easy for a smart girl like you to set it up without raising any eyebrows. Nod if we're still on the same page here."

Lexie nodded. Dylan held his gaze on her, searching her eyes to make certain that she wasn't shining him on. When he was satisfied that she understood the gravity of the situation and that his demands were deadly serious, he continued.

"And that's the end of her involvement. You tell her that. She doesn't check up on Beto, doesn't become his benefactor or try to be his 'second grandma' so she can have a link to me. I won't be around. But I will be watching. She just puts the money in and walks away—you won't have to explain that part to her; she already knows how to do it, she's had a lot of practice. You just give her the overview. Are we clear on this?"

Lexie nodded again.

"Once Charlie's done with his therapy and Beto has his degree, I'll erase this email and forget that I have an older half-brother stupid enough to send it to me in the first place. You tell her I said that. Tell her what my eyes looked like when I said it." He paused to let her take in his eyes. "And if she deviates from the deal—one single iota—I'll make her wish her crazy son had never met the Swedish underwear model on that 'business trip' to Malmö twenty-two years ago."

The look in Dylan's eyes didn't frighten Lexie, but it spoke to a place deep inside of her that she'd long thought lost. A place that had once overspilled with the quixotic dreams of a fifteen-year-old girl who actually believed in clichés like "hope springs eternal" and "true love" and "happily ever after."

She caught herself just before the ghostly tendrils of

that forgotten place inside her heart could take hold and draw her back into its warm embrace. And with a precise nod and cool gaze that came dangerously close to replicating a younger Ilona Kingley, she queried, "Is there anything else you require?"

Dylan held her gaze as he pushed back against the sole remaining unresolved issue on his mind.

But in the end, the urge was too strong to resist. He simply had to know.

As the image of the anonymous love letter that he had found in his high school locker surfaced against the backdrop of his memory, he asked, "Did you write that note?"

Lexie hesitated, and for a heartbreaking moment, she considered lying. Then with a scarcely perceptible movement of her head, she said softly, "I wish I had."

Dylan nodded with a sad smile. "That's too bad . . . I think I could have fallen in love with that girl."

EPILOGUE

The view of the city lights after dark was breathtaking, especially from the skydeck of the Hotel Valdéz—and particularly through the eyes of the eight-year-old boy up on his father's shoulders.

"Whoa!" Damián cried out with excitement. "Did you see that, Dad?"

Dylan smiled and said, "Yep. I saw it, buddy."

The line of blue light projected onto the left side of the Wilshire Grand Center had crept up another few inches, surpassing the line of red light on the right side of the building.

"Can I stay up to see it go all the way to the top, Dad?"

The boy's body was coursing with energy, but Dylan remained calm. The blue and red lights, which indicated the winner of individual states, were more ceremonial than practical. What mattered was the raw vote—or what was once quaintly referred to as the "popular vote," back when a handful of party-appointed state electors known as the "electoral college" decided the outcome. But that inequitable

191

system had long since been retired. When the final projected raw vote came in, one of the two lights would rise to the top of the Wilshire Grand, indicating the winner. But judging by the overwhelming turnout and slow returns in states where the polls had already closed, Dylan guessed it was going to be a while before the winning light ascended to the top of the shiny skyscraper across the way.

"Can I, Dad?" Damián asked again. "Can I stay up to see the light go to the top?"

"We'll have to ask Mom."

The boy laughed. "But you're the *governor*, Dad!"

Dylan smiled. "I am?"

The boy laughed harder. "Yes. You're the boss of all of California!"

"Yeah, but Mommy's the boss of me."

Damián stopped laughing. "Yeah, but *she* didn't get *elected*. *You* did. What you say *goes*."

"I don't think it works that way, buddy. Mommy's the boss at home. I'm just the boss at the state capitol—and even there, I work for the people."

Damián giggled like that was the silliest thing ever. "The *people* can't tell me when to go to bed."

"Yeah, but Mommy can."

Damián was thoughtful for a moment. And then he said, "But she's only the boss at home, right?" He looked at his father's reflection in the darkened pane of glass. "She's not the boss at work, right?"

He was a far more clever boy than Dylan was at eight, and his mind was constantly working, running down every possible angle of any dilemma, searching out the solution. His deep hazel eyes weren't fully lit yet, but there was a spark in them and more than enough kindling to catch fire.

Dylan smiled. "Proceed, counselor . . . "

Damián giggled. He liked it when his father played along. "The White House is like work *and* home, right? The West Wing is the work part, and the East Wing is the home part. So when you become president, Mommy only gets to be the boss of the East Wing, right?"

It was a fairly astute assessment, but Dylan waited for the kicker.

"But she only gets to be the boss of the East Wing *after* the inauguration, 'cause that's when you become the official president, right?"

Dylan concurred, with a measure of reservation.

"But *before* the inauguration," Damián went on, "you're the president-elect for almost three whole months, and you get to make *all* the decisions, like who's gonna be your chief of staff and who's gonna run the transition and who's gonna be in your cabinet, and no one can tell you no, except for the Senate because they're a separate yet equal branch of the government, and they have to confirm your cabinet, but for everything else you're the boss and no one else, right? So, if you win tonight, you'll be president-elect, and you can let me stay up without Mommy's permission."

Dylan smiled, marveling not only at the amount of information that could be absorbed by such a young mind but also at the skillful way his eight-year-old son had painted him into a corner.

"OK," Dylan said. "If I win, you can stay up."

Damián blinked, surprised that his line of reasoning had worked so easily. Dylan laughed, but as he looked past the skyscraper with the blue and red lights slowly climbing its façade, toward the backdrop of the night, where the mountains stood tall and dark, he felt uncertainty creeping in.

Damián was fast asleep by nine-thirty, and Dylan carried him to the bedroom where Brisa was already tucked in. It had been a very long day, and the end didn't appear to be in sight. He passed through the living room of the suite, where the top members of his campaign team were gathered around the TV, intently watching as the returns came in. Live shots of the convention hall on the mezzanine of the Valdéz displayed a massive crowd of supporters who appeared to be in high spirits.

On his way to the bedroom at the far end of the suite, Dylan passed Beto Larracuente, who had served in his gubernatorial cabinet as State Treasurer and throughout this campaign as his Chief Economics Advisor. Beto gave him a nod with a confident thumbs-up. Dylan returned the nod but without the thumbs-up. The polls had tightened to a razor-thin margin in several key populous states over the past few weeks, and nothing was guaranteed.

A single night light illuminated the bedroom, where Brisa lay curled up and fast asleep on the king-size bed. When Dylan pulled back the covers on the left side of the bed, Damián's eyes opened briefly, but the moment his cheek sank into the pillow, he fell right back to sleep. Dylan tucked him under the blanket and kissed him on the cheek.

He wanted to give Brisa a kiss too but didn't want to disturb her sleep. At six, Brisa was a light sleeper, and like her older brother, she had an inquisitive mind that worked overtime. If he woke her now, she might not be able to get back to sleep. It would likely be hours before the final result came in. If he won the election, he'd have to wake them for his acceptance speech down in the convention hall. But for now, he just wanted them to get a much-needed break from the whirlwind of activity that had become their lives over the past twenty months.

Dylan was about to leave the room when the large slumbering dog curled up on the bed between his sleeping children stirred and began to thump his bushy tail. Dylan held up a hand to still the dog's excitement, but it was too late. Brisa opened her eyes and smiled, and at once Dylan's heart melted.

He went around to her side of the bed and sat on the edge, fixing the large dog with a glance. The dog buried his face in shame, and Dylan ruffled his fur to let him know that he wasn't really angry. The tail began to thump again. Dylan looked into Brisa's eyes, which were beautiful and brown like her mother's. He stroked her long dark hair and said softly, "What are you doing up, Mija?"

"I had a dream."

"Was it a good dream?"

Brisa hesitated. "I can't remember."

Dylan smiled. "Well, that's how dreams are sometimes, sweetheart."

Brisa thought for a moment and then said, "I think I remember now."

Dylan nodded with a gentle smile. "OK."

Brisa searched his eyes; sincerity was an absolute necessity when she was going to share her intimate thoughts. Finding no guile in her father's eyes, she went on. "I was dreaming about the house by the water. The big house with the garden and the maze . . . the Winter White House . . . Do you remember it, Daddy?"

Dylan nodded. They had visited Largo Morta while campaigning in Florida back in June; this was shortly after Dylan had clinched the Democratic nomination for the presidency. Grandmama Lona had wanted to see her great-grandchildren. Charlie wasn't there, but Lexie was. And their son was too. He was a tall fourteen-year-old, with a lean yet athletic frame, whose features leaned more toward his mother than his father. His name was Dane. Lexie said that she and Charlie had given him this name to honor Grandmama Lona's long deceased and beloved younger brother, but Dylan suspected that Grandmama Lona had been an active participant in the naming of her first male grandchild.

Damián and Brisa had instantly fallen in love with their older cousin, and Dane had returned their affection, tirelessly playing with them in the garden and the pool, and then watching movies with them well into the night. And the following day, while Dylan and Mari-lynn were saying their goodbyes to Lexie and Grandmama Lona in the circular drive outside of the residence, Dane came out with Brisa in his arms and Damián up on his shoulders, both of them asking their parents if Dane could come with them. The tall boy with the deep blue eyes and shaggy blond hair had smiled bashfully at the unexpected outburst from his cousins, and in that moment Dylan felt an odd wave of tendrils race his spine. It wasn't déjà vu. It was something more concrete, something deeper. And without warning, Dylan found himself ready to say, "Sure, if he wants to."

It had been an impulsive reaction that for some reason felt completely natural to him. But Grandmama Lona had stepped in before Dylan could respond and explained kindly to the children that right now Dane needed to be with his mother and father, just as they needed to be with their mother and father. After the election was done, she added, they would all be able to spend more time together, and wouldn't that be wonderful . . .

But Dylan had only half heard his grandmother. He was looking at Dane as if for the first time. And when the boy came in for a goodbye hug, Dylan breathed him in. The embrace lasted long enough that Lexie began to feel uncomfortable, but Grandmama Lona, at ninety-one, stood tall and unshaken, with her chin held high.

When they finally parted, there were tears in the boy's eyes, and Dylan held the back of his neck in a reassuring grasp as he looked Dane in the eye and said softly yet resolutely, "We're gonna see you again. I promise. No matter what, we're gonna see you soon. We're family. OK?"

The boy nodded. A single tear rolled down his cheek, and Dylan wiped it away with a gentle movement of his thumb.

Brisa touched Dylan's cheek with her tiny fingers, and he came back to the present in the hotel bedroom, where the soft night light on the bedside table illuminated his daughter's lovely face.

"I was looking for you in the maze because you were lost, Daddy."

Dylan kissed her fingertips. "I'm right here, baby."

"I know that," Brisa said. "But in my dream, you were lost in the maze. You were looking for someone, and you got lost, and I was scared for you, but I couldn't find you."

Dylan had thought back on that night—the night he'd been lost in the maze at Largo Morta—countless times since. And he'd believed that he had found all that Charlie had hidden between the rows of tall hedges. But now, nearly sixteen years later, he wasn't quite so sure. Had there been something else Charlie had hidden? Something that Dylan couldn't possibly have found because it was *outside* of the maze?

She's not a flower, Dylan. She doesn't need your protection.

Those words came at him with a vengeance and were followed fast by others more telling.

You think you can have her without me?

I gave her to you, and I can take her back!

Charlie and Lexie's engagement had been announced in March of that year, and their marriage had taken place a month later. It had been a private ceremony, held at Largo Morta. Dylan hadn't been invited. And in mid-November, they had announced the birth of a baby boy, Dane Matthew Latner. Dylan had been touched that they'd given their son his middle name, and he'd sent a gift: a plush toy soccer ball, just like the one he'd picked out for Charlie after Charlotte had given birth to him. Lexie sent a thank you note, along with a photo of the baby snuggling up to the soft toy. The note read: "He won't go to sleep without it!" This was followed by several hearts, drawn in Lexie's flowing script.

Dylan had sent a gift every year on the boy's birthday, and Lexie had responded to each with a card. Even after

Dane had taken over the responsibility of writing his own thank you notes, Lexie always wrote a little something at the bottom before dropping the cards in the mail. Though they rarely saw each other in person (something always seemed to come up on Charlie and Lexie's end whenever Dylan suggested a get-together), Dane kept in contact with his uncle through social media, texts, and phone calls, and no matter how busy his schedule, Dylan always made the time to chat. Dane sent him videos of his soccer games and swim meets, and though they lived at opposite ends of the country, every now and then Dylan managed to attend one of his nephew's sporting events. On these rare occasions, Charlie was never present.

Dylan thought about that night with Lexie. The only time they'd been together. New Year's Eve. Nearly sixteen years ago. He could still hear her voice whispering in his ear as they reclined on his bed: *It's OK, I've got it covered.*

He thought about Dane, who was less than two weeks away from his fifteenth birthday. He thought about how easy it would be to change a birth certificate from mid-October to mid-November . . . if you were a person of means and without compunction, of course.

He could hear the three of them now, Lexie, Charlie, and Grandmama Lona, all taking turns at him:

I work for your grandmother . . . it's sort of an internship.

You think this makes you the winner, but you're wrong.

For a time I'd thought you might be the one. You have the stature, the natural appeal, and certainly the looks.

If it makes any difference, I would have spent the night with you anyway.

You think you're going to walk off into the sunset and have a happy ending? Not this time, Dylan.

You lack the killer instinct, dear . . . your heart is too pure and gentle.

Brisa's tiny fingers touched Dylan's cheek again, and

he kissed them again and smiled to let her know that everything was all right. But Brisa looked deep in thought. "Daddy," she said carefully, "are you the sexiest man alive?"

It never failed to surprise Dylan how quickly she could shift from one subject to an entirely different one. But he was glad her mind was off the dream about the maze.

"No, I'm not, honey," he said with a smile. "Michelangelo DiCaprio is."

Brisa looked both surprised and curious at once. "Who is Michelangelo DiCaprio?"

"He's the grandson of a very famous actor from a long time ago—back in your great-grandma's time. You saw him in that movie, the one with the ducks, remember?"

"Oh," Brisa said, but Dylan could tell that she was still thinking about her initial question.

"You liked that movie. Remember? He played the guy who saves the ducks."

"Yes," Brisa said. "He's very cute. But he's a *boy*, and the magazine said that you're the sexiest *man* alive."

Dylan's eyes narrowed, but he was still smiling. "Where is this headed?"

Usually Brisa couldn't resist a giggle when her daddy gave her his inquisitive smile—indeed it was her very favorite of all of his smiles. But she looked serious now. "I was just wondering because . . . because if you're the sexiest man alive, then you're the sexiest governor too, but the man on the news said that the president shouldn't be sexy, so if you get elected, will you be the sexiest president alive?"

Dylan looked into her sincere eyes. Sometimes a single look from her could take his breath away. He kissed her forehead and said softly, "We'll figure that out in the morning, OK?"

She surprised him by accepting his answer with a sweetly whispered "OK." And within moments of his gentle kiss on her forehead, she drifted off to sleep.

. . .

Phil Parma, Dylan's campaign manager, was waiting for him in the short hallway just outside the bedroom. He spoke in a soft voice so as not to disturb the sleeping children.

"We got clobbered in Ohio—no surprise there—and Florida keeps pulling votes out of its magic asshole, as usual. But on the upside, our worthy opponent has squeezed just about all he can get out of the bible belt, and the well has pretty much run dry in Texas too. We're not at the finish line, but we're pulling into the final lap. This one's yours to lose, buddy." He stopped and held up a hand. "Let me rephrase that: It's tight, but you're the odds on favorite as of—" He consulted his wristwatch. "—nine-forty-six, pacific time." He paused and then added. "If he doesn't contest, we could see a concession by eleven-thirty."

By nature, Dylan was a cautiously optimistic candidate and preferred not to entertain the odds, particularly in a tight race. But Phil, who had guided him to the governor's mansion, was an exceptional oddsmaker, who tirelessly combed through piles of polling data and knew every last county, district, and parish where votes could be squeezed out for a victory. And even more important, he knew precisely where an opponent's support was the weakest and just how to flip "soft voters."

Phil clapped a hand on Dylan's shoulder. "I know you don't like to count the chickens before they're cluckin', but I think we got this one, buddy." Phil looked at the bed, where the huge dog lay between the two sleeping kids. "Who needs Secret Service when you've got Chomper?" He chuckled. "Jesus, how old is he now?"

"He'll be seventeen next month."

Phil shook his head, smiling in amazement. "And her majesty—I take it she's prowling around here somewhere—how old is she now?"

"Twenty-two."

"Jesus," Phil chuckled in awe. "You shouldn't be president, you should be Dr. Dolittle."

Phil felt a familiar brushing sensation against his leg and looked down. The large Norwegian Forest cat gazed up at him languidly, and he petted her head. She purred in response and then leapt gracefully onto the bed.

Phil chuckled again. "You know she never forgave you for stealing her cat. Your old man was overjoyed. Didn't stop him from filing that lawsuit, of course, but that was only because he got tired of hearing Morgana bitch about it. How'd that ever turn out? Did he win?"

Dylan shook his head. "He dropped it."

Phil's eyes lit with understanding, and he grinned. "Ah, the hand of Grandmama Lona is far-reaching." He sighed. "My god, what is she like a hundred now?"

"Ninety-one."

"There is no rest for the wicked." With a nod to the bed, where Akasha was curling up against Hakhan, Phil added, "What do you suppose that is in cat years?"

Dylan laughed.

Phil sighed, looking at Akasha again. "She'd have never made it past ten if you'd left her there—not with your old man skulking around." He grinned. "But still, I'd have never figured you for a cat burglar—literally."

Dylan shrugged. "It was a spur of the moment thing." And with a smile, he added, "And as I recall, I couldn't have done it without my accomplice."

This was true. Had Phil Parma not been at the right place at the right time, Akasha would likely not be here now. But as it turned out, luck had been on the side of the clever Norwegian Forest cat on that sunny mid-morning at Largo Morta almost sixteen years ago.

Dylan remembered the scene as if it were yesterday. He had just backed his Tesla Roadster out of the private carport and was heading for the main drive when Hakhan suddenly jumped up and, planting his front paws on the edge of the passenger side door, began to bark. Dylan hit the break at once, fearing that Hakhan might leap from the moving convertible. At first, he couldn't see what the dog was barking at and assumed it was a squirrel or some other small animal hiding in the bushes near the residence. Hakhan loved to chase all outdoor animals, especially squirrels. He never caught any of them and probably wouldn't know what to do if he had, but he loved the pursuit.

But this time, the huge Alsatian had made no attempt at pursuit. He just kept barking at the residence and intermittently turning to Dylan with a pleading whine until Dylan finally saw what he was seeing. There across the lawn between the driveway and the residence, Akasha stood inside the old man's office, gazing out at Dylan and Hakhan. When she caught Dylan's eye, her ears perked up, and, standing on her hind legs, she began to paw at the mullioned glass panes of the French doors. The old man was at his desk, reading the riot act to Brady and Tom. Hakhan looked at Dylan and released a pitiful whine as his tail wagged hopefully, but there was no way Dylan could get to the French doors and open them without being noticed.

And then Phil had appeared. He was looking down at an open file in one hand while sipping a cup of coffee. Without pausing from his reading, Phil set the coffee mug on the corner of the old man's desk and then casually turned to the French doors. With her paws still up on the glass panes, Akasha looked up at Phil. Without breaking from his perusal of the file, Phil petted the cat's head and then opened one of the doors—just enough so that she could slip outside. It was all done so smoothly that no one else in the office even noticed. As Akasha dashed across the lawn to Dylan's car, Dylan thought he saw Phil drop a surreptitious wink before turning back to the desk to retrieve his coffee mug.

Phil was grinning at Dylan now in the darkened hallway of the hotel suite. "Yeah, well, nobody was ever able to prove collusion between us on that one, so let's keep it on the QT. I've already pissed off enough members of your family. No need to add Morgana to the list—her vengeance has no expiration date." He patted Dylan's arm. "Come take a look at your speech after you're done here."

Dylan stood in the doorway of the bedroom for a while longer. No thoughts of the election outcome, no worries over the past. He just stood there, watching his children sleep, and for the first time in a long time, he felt at peace.

The TV pundits were fired up, and the campaign staffers in the living room of the opulent suite watched with rapt attention as Colin Grimley channeled the spirit of his father, the late great Chase Grimley, for his fellow pundits gathered at the NCMSB news desk in the New York studio. "Either way this goes down, two things are absolutely locked in and one hundred percent guaranteed.

"Number one, we're about to get our youngest president ever, period. It's either gonna be the thirty-two-year-old fire-and-brimstone, pull-no-punches, party-hardliner Republican candidate from the state of New York *or* the thirty-seven-year-old soft-spoken, no-nonsense, actions-speak-louder-than-words, hopeful pragmatist Democratic candidate from the state of California. That's history in the making right there, I'm telling you.

"And *this* guy—the California governor—knows of what he speaks! Or practices what he preaches. Or whatever other colloquialism you wanna use to describe the great things he's done for the state of California over the past eight years as their governor. At twenty-nine, he became the youngest ever elected, beating out the previous record holder J. Neely Johnson, who was thirty when he became the fourth governor of the Golden State back in 1856—how's that for a history lesson? Ha!

"But the difference is, Cali's *current* governor isn't a limp

Whig who couldn't muster enough support to hold the office beyond two years. He's a bona fide two-term champion of the people with real class and dignity—and he doesn't have to raise his voice to be heard. He's the genuine article, and the voters see it. They can *feel* it. This guy actually *cares* about them." He paused and then added with a grin, "And his matinee idol good looks don't hurt him, either, I suppose."

The crowd around the TV cheered and whistled, and Dylan, who had just entered the living room unnoticed, smiled when one of his campaign pollsters called out to the screen, "You tell 'em, Grimley!"

Colin Grimley went on. "The second thing that's already written into the history books is that the surname of the next President of the United States of America—all fifty-six of them—is going to be *Latner*.

"Because that's what we've got here, for the first time ever, two brothers—from the same father, with different mothers, but brothers nonetheless—are the nominees selected by the Dems and the GOP, and they couldn't be more different in politics or presentation. And if it's the *younger* brother, Charlie, the Republican candidate, who emerges victorious, it'll be a real twist of irony because he'll have the *Democratic* Ocasio-Cortez Amendment to thank for it—the Amendment that lowered the age requirement for president from thirty-five to thirty. If he wins this thing tonight, he'll take the oath of office one month before his thirty-third birthday.

"Either way, what a spectacular run this has been! The great-grandsons of a former president—albeit a disgraced one, no spoilers there. And yet out of the ashes of that fallen political empire—if you could call it an empire, that is—these two young phoenixes rise on opposite sides of the political spectrum to win their respective parties' nominations. You can't make this stuff up! I'm serious! This is like some Shakespearean drama of old. I'm talking epic Clash of the Titans-style drama, with the sons of Zeus going at it for the throne of Mount Olympus! Or maybe it's more like Thor and Loki, the sons of Odin in that old movie. Remember that one? What a classic!

"Add to that the burning question that's on everybody's mind: with a race this tight and hard-fought, when the final vote tally comes in, will there be a concession from one of these brothers tonight? I'm serious! This has been a hellava race. A real old-fashioned nail-biter, right down to the wire. I'm not kidding. This race has had *everything*, from rumors of a stolen family cat to a battle with bows and arrows down at Largo Morta in Florida! You just can't make this stuff up!

"Either way, this is some real drama, and it's happening live, tonight, right here on NCMSB, where, in the next hour or so, we expect to find out which of these brothers is going to be the next President of the United States . . . "

Colin Grimley ended up being wrong on those last two counts.

The final vote tally ended up coming in less than a half hour later. And the concession call was made shortly thereafter.

Dylan stood alone in the skydeck, his mobile phone to his ear, his gaze locked on the single strip of color that ran to the top of the Wilshire Grand, indicating the winner of the election. For a long moment, there was silence on both ends of the line.

Then Charlie spoke. "I know how hard this is for you Dylan, and I would do anything I could to make it easier on you. I honestly would. You spent over half your life protecting me, and I never got around to telling you how much that meant to me. It really did. But now you can't protect me anymore. You understand that, don't you?"

Dylan nodded, unable to speak. But somehow he knew that Charlie could feel his unspoken response.

Another long moment passed. And it was Charlie who spoke again. And what he said was unexpected but not surprising.

"He's gone," Charlie said. "Dane. He left sometime this morning—slipped his Secret Service detail." He exhaled a breath that sounded like a soft laugh. "He's mastered the old slip maneuver and is every bit as good at it as you were at his age."

This time Charlie's laugh came through clearly, and there was no mistaking the admiration in it. Dylan tried to return the laugh in camaraderie, but the best he could manage was a small sad smile. He remained silent as he gazed at the line of light that stretched all the way to the top of the building across the dark sky.

"In any case," Charlie went on, "I expect you'll be seeing him soon. He was on a four-thirty flight, with a stopover in Vegas. The connecting flight was delayed, but it landed in LA about an hour ago so you should alert your Secret Service detail." A brief pause. "I don't want him wandering the streets." Another pause, longer this time. "He should be with you. Especially tonight."

Dylan turned and looked over his shoulder. Through the glass doors which opened into the living room, he could see the tall blond boy entering the suite, with his eyes down as if trying to blend into the crowd. He didn't get far before Mari-lynn spotted him and took him into a warm embrace as if he were her own child. They had never discussed what both of them had long suspected, but Dylan knew that his wife would have no reservations if the day ever came when Dane showed up at their door.

Dylan spoke into the phone. "He's here. He just walked through the door."

A moment passed, and then Charlie said, "I'm glad to hear he got there safely."

206

Dylan nodded. "He's safe."

Charlie made a soft sound in his throat and then said, "I think he should stay with you for a while, Dylan. I know that's a lot to ask of you, especially considering the night's outcome, but—" He took a short breath, and Dylan could almost see him raising his chin in that regal manner. "I really think that's what's best for him right now. And I would appreciate it if you would attend to him as if he was your own."

Dylan nodded and said softly, "I will."

A long silence followed, in which neither of the brothers spoke.

As before, it was Charlie who broke the silence.

"Well, then," Charlie said briskly, "I suppose there's only one thing left for me to say—and it's my honor and privilege to be the first to say it: Congratulations, Mr. President-elect."